SAY YES TO A SECOND CHANCE

CINDY KIRK

WAVERLY
HOUSE

ISBN: 9798607790868

First published in 2013 as A JACKSON HOLE HOMECOMING by Silhouette Books

CHAPTER ONE

Adrianna Lee took a step back, her heart in her throat. As a nurse midwife, watching parents ooh and aah over their little one was her favorite part of the birthing process.

This time had been extra special because the baby she'd delivered was the new son of her friends Betsy and Ryan Harcourt. Seeing Ryan's dark head pressed against Betsy's blond strands as they carefully checked out their new son's fingers and toes brought a quiver of longing.

When would it be her turn? When would she find a man to love and stand by her? A man eager to build a life with her? She'd imagined the scenario many times. But the man in her dreams wasn't some faceless entity. He had a face. And a name. Tripp Randall.

There was only one little problem. Okay, one *big* problem. He wasn't interested in her.

"I heard the good news."

Adrianna turned toward the deep voice and there he stood. The man who'd captured her heart at fourteen by gallantly carrying some branches to the curb for her. At the time he'd been a hunky seventeen-year-old capable of turning her knees to mush with a single glance. As the steady boyfriend of her neighbor, he'd also been unattainable.

These days he was the CEO of the Jackson Hole Hospital, a widower and *still* unattainable.

Tripp stepped close, keeping his voice low, as if not wanting to disturb the sleeping baby nestled in Betsy's arms. "How did everything go?"

"Perfect." Adrianna couldn't keep the pride from her voice. "He's a healthy eight-pound-six-ounce boy and Betsy barely broke a sweat."

"So not true," Betsy called out from the rocker. "Trust me, there's a good reason it's called labor."

Her dark-haired husband brushed a strand of hair back from his wife's face, his eyes filled with concern. "I didn't like seeing you in such pain. Even when Adrianna assured me everything was proceeding normally, I worried."

Beside her, Adrianna felt Tripp stiffen. Pregnancy was a natural occurrence but not without risk. Tripp knew that better than most. He'd lost his wife, Gayle, and their unborn baby three years ago when the placenta had abruptly separated from the uterine wall. Adrianna raised her hand to touch his arm in a comforting gesture but pulled back at the last second.

Tripp rarely spoke of his loss. Adrianna remembered the moment she'd heard the news as if it were yesterday.

"I'm happy for you both," she heard Tripp say. If there was any inner turmoil, his voice gave nothing away. "Have you decided on a name?"

"Nathan." Betsy's radiant smile lit up the entire room. "It means 'he whom God has given.'"

"Nate Harcourt." Tripp cocked his head and appeared to roll the name around on his tongue. "I like it. Great name for a bull rider."

Ryan had been a champion bull rider before hanging up his spurs to attend law school.

Betsy's mouth widened in a perfect O and she glanced at her husband in horror. Obviously the thought of her baby boy one day straddling the back of a big bad bull didn't sit well with the new mom.

Ryan shot Tripp a glinting "you'll pay for that comment" before patting his wife's shoulder. "No need to think of that now, sweetheart. That's a lot of years away."

"C'mon." This time, Adrianna let her fingers curve around Tripp's arm. "You've caused enough trouble for one day. Let's give Betsy and Ryan time alone with their son."

Tripp managed to call out his congratulations before Adrianna pulled him into the hall and shut the door to the birthing suite behind them.

"Hey, if you wanted to get me alone all you had to do was ask."

The devilish twinkle in his eyes brought a smile to Adrianna's lips and made her forget the scolding words on her tongue.

The man had the soul of a mischievous imp. Not to mention he was too attractive for his own good. His collar-length hair was artfully disheveled, the blond waves practically inviting a woman's fingers to slide through the soft strands. The patch of scruff on his chin only added to his appeal.

Whenever she saw Tripp at Wally's Place—a popular local bar —dressed in jeans and boots with his fingers curved around a bottle of Dos Equis, it was hard to imagine he could be the CEO of a health system with a multimillion-dollar budget. But his performance spoke for itself. Even though he'd been in the position for less than a year, he'd already garnered praise for his innovative changes.

They'd barely stepped away from the door when a nurse approached Adrianna for her signature. As she scrawled her name on the prescription, Adrianna couldn't help noticing the pretty redhead checking out Tripp.

"We don't see you up on the Maternity floor much, Mr.

Randall." The recently divorced nurse gazed at him through lowered lashes.

The RN clearly had the CEO in her crosshairs. Adrianna understood the appeal. Not only was Tripp wearing her favorite beige Armani suit with the blue tie that matched his eyes, but he also smelled terrific. A woman could get intoxicated simply breathing in the spicy scent of his cologne.

"What brings you up here today?" The nurse shifted from one foot to the other, clearly in no hurry to get back to her patients.

"Some friends had a baby." He slanted a smile in Adrianna's direction. "And I have a proposition for Ms. Lee."

A look of disappointment skittered across the nurse's face, but Tripp didn't appear to notice.

"Well, if I can ever be of service to you, don't hesitate to call me."

There was a decidedly suggestive undertone to the nurse's words that would be hard to miss, but Tripp's easy smile never wavered.

"I'll keep that in mind—" he glanced at her name tag "—Lila."

"It's Leila," the redhead corrected, then frowned as another nurse motioned to her from the doorway of one of the birthing suites. Still, she offered Tripp another smile before strolling off, her hips swinging from side to side.

Adrianna fought an unexpected surge of jealousy. She waited until Leila was out of earshot, then took out her irritation on him. "*Proposition?* Couldn't you think of a less suggestive word? The nurse probably thinks you want to sleep with me."

His eyes widened.

Adrianna stifled a groan. Talk about a Freudian slip.

"Nah." Tripp finally waved a dismissive hand. "Everyone knows we're just friends."

The words had barely left his lips when Adrianna's phone pinged. She slipped it from her pocket and glanced down. A patient she'd been following had been admitted in labor.

"If you have a proposition for me, you'd better spit it out quick." Adrianna softened her abruptness with a smile. "I've got to run."

"The hospital fundraiser at the Spring Gulch Country Club is Saturday." Tripp shoved his hands in his pockets and rocked back on his heels. "The way I figure, it makes sense for us to go together."

"You're asking me to go with you? Why?" Adrianna didn't bother to curb her bluntness. She and Tripp had been down this road many times since he'd returned to Jackson Hole.

Even though neither could deny the curious energy between them, he'd made it clear on many occasions that he had zero romantic interest in her. The last time the subject had come up she'd lied and said she felt the same way about him.

"I have to be there. You have to be there." His tone turned persuasive. "We might as well go together."

What he said made sense as far as it went. His was a command performance. As a member of the medical staff, her attendance at the annual fundraising dinner and dance was highly encouraged.

There were any number of women in Jackson Hole who'd be happy to be his date.

"Why me?" she asked, puzzled. "Why not ask someone else? Someone who appeals to you?"

Merely saying the words brought a pang of regret. They could be so good together...if he'd just give her a chance.

"You're a beautiful woman." Tripp spoke quickly as she began edging her way down the hall. "Any man would be proud to have you by his side."

Adrianna stopped and fisted her hands on her hips. "You didn't answer my question."

This time Tripp didn't pretend to misunderstand. "With you there'd be no expectations. I could network without worrying I'm neglecting you. You could do the same. Don't we have fun when we're together?"

Adrianna reluctantly nodded. Yes, they always had fun. Yes, she enjoyed being with him, but that was no longer enough. Last week she'd looked at the calendar and realized she'd turn thirty in a few weeks. She'd hoped that by this point she'd have a husband and a couple of kids.

That wasn't going to happen if she kept hanging around Tripp Randall. She *must* tell him no. After all, there were bound to be lots of single men at the event. There was no point in attending the function with Tripp, a man who'd made his feelings very clear. Unless...

"I'll go." Adrianna's heart skipped a beat at the smile he shot her. "On one condition."

He took her hand and brought it to his lips. "Whatever you want."

She ignored the tingles shooting up her arm and met his gaze. "You have to promise to introduce me to all your single friends."

~

Tripp ran a finger along the starched inside collar of his shirt and wondered why—just once—the hospital couldn't host a fundraiser where jeans and boots were de rigueur instead of formal attire.

Pick your battles, he told himself, and refocused on the solil-oquy—er, conversation—that had been going on for endless minutes. When the portly gray-haired rancher—who happened to also be one of the trustees on the hospital board—paused after finishing a rather lengthy review of his Hereford breeding program, Tripp stuck out his hand. "Stop by my office anytime, Paul. Let me know how that new bull works out."

Even though Tripp had been away from horses and cattle for many years, the fact that he'd grown up working on his father's land gave him an automatic "in" with many in the community, especially those involved in ranching.

When Tripp decided to return, it was his MBA in Healthcare Leadership at Yale and almost ten years of experience in healthcare policy and economics that had made him a viable candidate for the CEO position.

"Mark my words, that bull will—"

"I think Tripp knows exactly what the bull will do. Let the boy get back to his date." Paul's wife pointed to some friends across the room and insisted her husband come with her to say hello.

"Nice to see you again, Marie," Tripp called out as she took her husband's arm in a steely grasp and they disappeared into the crowd.

Tripp snagged a glass of wine from a passing waiter and took a sip, surveying the large room. The Spring Gulch Country Club was where most hospital events were held and this year's fundraiser for pediatric monitoring equipment was no exception.

Tables with silent-auction items filled the perimeter of a large room just off the country club's foyer. A huge rustic stone fireplace acted as the focal point for the room. Chandeliers made out of antlers hung from the angled ceiling. Even though the beautiful hardwood floors and the tables topped with linen screamed elegance, the chandeliers added a distinctly casual touch.

Huge urns of flowers surrounded the shiny wooden dance floor. Crystal goblets and sterling-silver flatware gleamed in the candlelight. Most of those in attendance, men in tuxedos and women in cocktail dresses, were people Tripp had known his entire life.

When he caught a glimpse of his parents on the dance floor and his mother gave him a tremulous smile, Tripp realized once again how good it was to be back. Even though the man who'd once herded cattle all day was now having difficulty slow dancing with his wife, the fact that his dad was here and steady on his feet brought a thankful lump to Tripp's throat.

While Tripp didn't regret his years on the East Coast, he did regret staying away so long.

His sister had grown from a girl into a woman while he'd been away. He caught sight of her dancing with one of Travis Fisher's younger brothers, a big smile on her face. Like him, Hailey loved to dance.

Tripp realized he hadn't been on the dance floor yet this evening. That could be easily remedied. Even though there were dozens of single women at tonight's event—including the red-haired maternity nurse, Leila—he would dance first with the woman he'd brought. He glanced around the ballroom until he spotted Adrianna walking with Lexi on the edge of the dance floor.

"You've got a good eye." A man's voice sounded from Tripp's left. "She's the prettiest filly in the stable."

Tripp turned. The man, standing with a glass of whiskey in one hand, was unfamiliar. Even though he had to be in his early thirties—which would make them close to the same age—he wasn't from Jackson Hole.

Tall, with an athletic build, the stranger had the confident stance of a person used to giving orders. His dark hair was cut stylishly short and the Hublot Black Caviar on his wrist hadn't come off the ten-dollar watch rack. But it was his steely gray eyes that defined him.

Tripp extended his hand. "I don't believe we've met. I'm Tripp Randall, the CEO of the Jackson Hole Hospital."

The man returned Tripp's handshake with an equally strong grasp. "Winston Ferris." He flashed a smile showing a mouthful of perfect white teeth. "Call me Winn."

"Are you new to Jackson Hole, Winn?"

"I am," Winn acknowledged, his eye shifting back to the dance floor. "My father has been here a couple of years."

Jim Ferris. One of the newer members on the hospital's board of trustees. And, according to Tripp's dad, the one who'd been most resistant to hiring him.

Tripp had already forgiven the man for his error in judgment.

After all, like his son said, Jim was relatively new to the community.

"Are you planning to stay?" Tripp didn't want to pry, but he was curious. Jim Ferris had recently outbid his father on the large cattle spread adjacent to their property.

"Haven't decided yet." Winn's eyes took on a lust-filled glow. "But if she'd give me a tumble, I'd definitely give more thought to hanging around."

Tripp shifted his gaze in the direction Winn stared. A group of women stood clustered together, laughing and talking. Any one of the beauties could have caught Winn's eye. Tripp knew instantly which "filly" stood out from the herd.

When he'd picked up Adrianna tonight, he'd taken one look at her and immediately thought of a thousand things he'd rather be doing than attending a fundraiser.

Things he shouldn't be thinking about a woman who was only a friend. A woman who'd been his wife's friend. Even if Tripp had been ready to date again—to get naked with a woman again—it wouldn't be with Adrianna. It would be with someone new, not with someone so deeply linked to his past.

Yet, he couldn't deny there was chemistry between them. Desire had hit him full force when he'd first seen her this evening. He'd had to restrain himself from pulling her into his arms and scattering kisses across her face and neck. From pulling the pins from her hair so he could run his fingers through the silky strands. From easing the dress from her shoulders and letting it fall to the floor—

"Who is she?"

Tripp jerked his thoughts back to the present. Even though he should be relieved—after all, he had no business thinking of Adrianna in that manner—he found himself irritated by the man's persistence.

"Which one?" Tripp forced a bored tone.

Winn snorted. "The hot brunette. She's a dead ringer for that Brazilian actress."

Tripp took a sip of wine. "Adrianna Lee. She's a nurse midwife."

"Is she married?"

Tripp didn't like the way Winn looked at Adrianna, as if she were a piece of meat and he hadn't eaten in a week.

There was no point in lying. Winn could easily discover the truth for himself. "She's not."

"The night is definitely looking up." Winn grinned. "One more question. Do you know if she's seeing anyone?"

Tripp thought of the promise he'd made to Adrianna. But Winn was a new acquaintance, certainly not a friend. And even if he was, she deserved better than a man who'd compare her to a horse.

"Do you know if she's seeing anyone?" Winn repeated, a determined glint in his gray eyes.

Tripp smiled. "As a matter of fact, she's with me."

CHAPTER TWO

Adrianna felt Tripp's gaze on her from clear across the ballroom. But then, being so aware of him was nothing new. She'd recently told her friend Betsy it was as if she had special "Tripp radar" hardwired into her system.

"Do you know the guy Tripp is speaking with?" she asked Lexi Delacourt, another dear friend and one of the most beautiful women in Jackson Hole.

Lexi obligingly shifted her attention across the room, missing the admiring glances sent her way by a couple of cowboy types walking past. Adrianna could see why the men were impressed. Her friend looked especially lovely this evening in an off-the-shoulder dress in crimson with her sleek dark hair hanging loosely to her shoulders.

Her husband, Nick, must have thought she looked appealing, too, because a few minutes earlier, on her way to the powder room to check her makeup, Adrianna had stumbled upon the two kissing. It hadn't been a simple peck on the lips either.

Lexi had been embarrassed, but Adrianna had told her she hoped when she finally married that her husband would find her irresistible enough to pull her into an alcove and kiss her with such passion.

"He's certainly handsome. Who could he be?" Lexi expelled a frustrated breath and pursed her red lips. Her friend prided herself on knowing most of the residents of Jackson Hole, but it looked as though this time she was coming up empty.

"Could he be someone's date?"

"It appears he's single. At least I don't *think* he's wearing a ring." As if to confirm her guess, the social worker narrowed her gaze, refocusing on his left hand.

"Ohmigod, Lex," Adrianna hissed. "He saw you staring and now both of them are headed this way."

The two men had begun to wind their way across the large ballroom, Tripp as fair as the other man was dark. Even though his friend was attractive, he didn't affect Adrianna in the slightest.

Not like Tripp. When she'd seen him in his black tux tonight, her heart rate had skyrocketed into the danger zone. It was the first time she'd seen him dressed so formally since his junior–senior prom. She'd watched him arrive in a limo to pick up Gayle. While the two were dancing and laughing in the high school gym, Adrianna had been up in her room eating a pint of Chunky Monkey ice cream.

"They're almost here," Lexi whispered, sounding more like a high school friend than a happily married woman and mother of two. "Stay cool. We'll pretend we don't see them."

"Is book club still on for this month?" Adrianna kept her gaze focused on Lexi.

"It is and we need to tell everyone that it's okay to come even if they haven't read *The Garden of Forking Paths.*"

Heat stole across Adrianna's cheeks. The upcoming selection had been Lexi's choice. Most of the group preferred genre fiction, but the social worker was determined to "broaden their horizons." She'd suggested *Adrianna Karenina,* but the members had all said they'd read it, though Adrianna suspected most of them hadn't.

At first, the short-story spy narrative appeared to be a more palatable solution. Until Adrianna went on to *Wikipedia* and discovered even the plot summary confused her.

"Borge's story is a good example of hypertext fiction," Adrianna murmured, repeating what she'd read in reviews.

From the smile lifting Lexi's lips, the observation must have been spot-on. "Exactly. That's why I wish the others would simply give it a—"

"Ladies." Tripp surprised Adrianna by not only kissing her cheek but by also slipping an arm around her shoulders. "I hope we're not interrupting."

Adrianna blinked, stunned by the proprietary gesture. For several seconds her voice vanished.

Lexi waved a dismissive hand. "Just book-club stuff. Nothing important."

The dark-haired man lifted a brow. "What's the book of the month?"

Lexi's smile broadened. "*The Garden of Forking Paths.* It's a short story by—"

"Jorge Luis Borge." The stranger finished the sentence for her. "An excellent example of hypertext fiction."

Lexi slanted a glance in Adrianna's direction. "That's what you just said."

"So you also liked the story?" Tripp's friend settled his steely gray eyes on Adrianna.

"It was okay." Now that he was close up, Adrianna admitted Lexi was right. He *was* handsome. And he had a confidence she found appealing. But so far, not a single spark.

Don't be hasty, she told herself. Attraction often needs time to build.

"I don't believe we've met," Lexi said politely when Tripp made no move to perform introductions. "I'm Lexi Delacourt and this is my friend Adrianna Lee."

"Winston Ferris." The man extended his hand. "But please call me Winn. Winston is far too formal."

"Is your wife here with you tonight, Mr.—er, Winn?" Lexi probed, her amber eyes sparkling with curiosity.

"I'm not married." Winn smiled. "Or dating anyone."

At that announcement, Lexi cast a pointed glance in Adrianna's direction, which she promptly ignored.

Thank goodness she hadn't yet told Lexi that she was ready to start looking for Mr. Right. If she had, there was no doubt in her mind that her friend would be shoving her in Winn's direction, despite the fact she was here tonight with Tripp.

"Ferris?" A frown furrowed Lexi's pretty brow. "Are you any relation to Jim?"

"He's my father." Winn may have answered Lexi, but his gaze remained firmly fixed on Adrianna.

"My husband, Nick, has golfed with your dad a few times." Lexi lifted her glass of wine to her lips. "I've heard your father has an amazing chip shot."

Winn simply smiled and refocused on Adrianna. "What about you? Do you have a husband? Or a boyfriend?"

Adrianna hesitated. While she supposed some might be flattered by his attention, his dogged determination to capture her interest rubbed her wrong, reminding her of that bad experience with her college boyfriend.

Besides, making a move on her wasn't particularly gentlemanly, considering she was here with someone else. *Unless* Tripp had told him they were only friends.

Adrianna slanted a sideways glance at Tripp, hoping for some answers.

"I thought I made it clear that Adrianna is with me." There was an undercurrent of warning running through Tripp's voice that surprised Adrianna.

Whatever she'd expected Tripp to say, it wasn't that. Was he aware by phrasing it that way it sounded as if they were a real couple?

"That's right." Winn gave a little laugh. "Must have slipped my mind."

Tripp's gaze shifted to Adrianna.

"It's past time we dance." He slipped his arm from her shoulder and took her hand. Before his fingers laced through hers, his thumb caressed her palm.

Adrianna's knees suddenly went weak.

Tripp smiled. There was warmth—dare she say, *heat?*—in his eyes that she couldn't recall seeing there before.

"Dancing would be...lovely." Her tongue moistened her suddenly dry lips and once again she saw a flash of heat.

"Nice to meet you, Winn," she called over her shoulder as Tripp tugged her to the dance floor, then jerked her close.

They fit as though they were made for each other. Tripp was just enough taller that even with her heels they came together perfectly. She wondered what it would be like if they made love. Would they come together just as perfectly? She promptly banished the thought. It wasn't as if that was ever going to happen.

Of course, she thought, resting her head against his broad chest, it wasn't as if she thought he'd ever hold her hand either. Or kiss her cheek.

Tripp's arms were so strong it didn't matter if her knees had the consistency of gelatin. When the band launched into a rendition of "Embraceable You," a special favorite of her parents, a sadness washed over Adrianna.

She'd been nineteen and away at college when her parents had passed away, victims of carbon monoxide poisoning due to a blocked fireplace flue. Adrianna lifted her head and gazed up at Tripp. "Did you know Gayle was the first person to express her condolences after my parents died?"

He shook his head, then frowned. "What made you think of that?"

"My mom and dad loved this song." Adrianna sighed, feeling a bit wistful. "Whenever it would come on the radio, they'd drop whatever they were doing and dance."

If she closed her eyes, she could see them now, her mother's head on her dad's shoulder, a dreamy smile on her lips.

"They'd been married for almost fifteen years and had given up hope of having any children when I came along," Adrianna continued. "A child in the house had to have been a big change, but I always felt wanted and loved."

Her troubles in college had occurred after their deaths. She'd been so lonely, so naive, so willing to believe a handsome man's lies. Then her world had imploded and she'd had no one. Adrianna told herself that, unlike her friends, her mom and dad would have stood by her through that horrible time.

How different things might have been...

Sighing again, she placed her cheek against the starched front of Tripp's shirt and let herself relax.

"Have you had a nice evening so far?" Tripp murmured against her hair.

"It's been fun." She lifted her head and realized with a start that his lips were right there. If she leaned forward ever so slightly, they would kiss. *Really* kiss.

Her heart stuttered.

The music disappeared.

Had she ever noticed the tiny gold flecks in his blue eyes? Or the faint smattering of freckles across the bridge of his nose? Or how good he smelled? Yes, she'd definitely noticed how good he smelled. Like soap. And sexy cologne. And that indefinable male scent that made something tighten deep in her abdomen.

Tripp's eyes darkened. His mouth drew closer.

Anticipation skittered up Adrianna's spine. She held her breath.

"You two look like you're having a good time."

Tripp stopped so abruptly that Adrianna stumbled.

"Are you okay?" he asked, after helping her regain her balance. She nodded.

"I'm sorry. We didn't mean to startle you."

Adrianna turned to find Tripp's parents staring at her.

"I'm fine. Really." Heat rose up her neck and she wondered how much they'd seen. Of course, it wasn't as if their son had actually *kissed* her.

"You look lovely this evening," Tripp's mother gushed. "Doesn't Adrianna look pretty, Frank?"

"Beautiful," Tripp's father responded.

Pleasure slid through Adrianna's veins like warm honey. She couldn't believe Tripp's mother remembered her, much less recalled her name. They'd met only once and that was months ago. "It's a pleasure to see both of you again, Mr. and Mrs. Randall."

"Please, call me Kathy." The sparkle in his mother's blue eyes reminded Adrianna of Tripp. She looked every inch a wealthy rancher's wife with her dark blond hair cut in a stylish bob and her elegant black dress brightened by large teardrop diamond earrings and a matching necklace.

Her husband stood beside her, one hand resting lightly on her back. A tall man with salt-and-pepper hair and a weathered face, Franklin had lost a lot of weight in the past year and his tux hung loosely on his large frame.

"Was that Jim Ferris's boy I saw you speaking with a few minutes ago?" Frank asked his son.

"His name is Winston." Tripp cupped Adrianna's elbow in his hand and they followed his parents off the dance floor. "From what he said, it sounds like he just got into town. He didn't mention if he planned on staying."

"Oh, he's staying." Frank gave a humorless chuckle. "He's in bed with GPG. The word is he was involved with golf-course development in Florida. Wants to do the same here and has GPG's backing."

GPG had been in the local news a lot lately. It was a large investment firm with deep pockets and a mission to develop every inch of Jackson Hole. Environmental concerns were simply obstacles to be overcome.

"GPG or no GPG, getting approval will be a problem." Tripp appeared pleased at the prospect. "Any golf-course development will have to meet the environmentally sensitive guidelines the county implemented last year."

"Golf." Adrianna wrinkled her nose. "I've never understood the point of hitting a little white ball."

Frank's eyes widened. He opened his mouth, then clamped it shut without responding.

Kathy looked amused.

Tripp chuckled.

"Considering my father used to practically live on the golf course, a statement like that is tantamount to waving a red flag in front of a bull," Tripp whispered in a tone loud enough for all of them to hear.

Warmth crept up Adrianna's neck but she lifted her chin. "It's just my opinion."

"And mine." Kathy shot Adrianna a wink.

Before much more could be said, an announcement sent them to their assigned seats for dinner.

Adrianna recognized two of the men and one of the women already at their table as being current board members. Although they were seniors, Adrianna wasn't worried. Because of her parents being older, she'd always felt comfortable with that generation. She chatted easily throughout a delicious meal of chicken, asparagus and wild rice. The dessert she left untouched.

"Is something wrong with the cheesecake?" Tripp leaned close, the question meant for her ears only.

Adrianna lifted one shoulder in a slight shrug and tried to pretend his nearness didn't affect her. "Simply too much food."

"No wine. No dessert. You're a cheap date," Tripp teased.

Her heart twisted. If only this *was* a real date....

"What are you thinking?" Tripp asked.

"That I'm having a nice time tonight."

"You sound surprised."

"In a way I am," she answered honestly. "For me, these events are normally just something to endure."

He brushed a stray tendril of hair back from her cheek with one finger. "You're having a good time tonight because you're with me."

Adrianna rolled her eyes while inwardly agreeing.

The band started up again and Adrianna found herself swaying with the music.

Tripp pushed back his chair.

When she stood and he took her hand, electricity shot up Adrianna's arm.

"I love the songs they're playing tonight—" she began, then stopped when Winn stepped in front of her.

The man smiled at Adrianna and ignored Tripp. "May I have the pleasure of this dance, Ms. Lee?"

Even though outwardly Winn appeared self-assured, something in his eyes told Adrianna he wasn't as confident as he appeared. She knew all about faking confidence in social settings. The knowledge that they had that in common made her offer him an extra-warm smile.

"The lady isn't available. She's dancing every dance with me." Tripp's blue eyes were positively frosty.

"Let her go with him, son." Jim Ferris seemed to appear out of nowhere. "There are several things I've been meaning to discuss with you. This will be a good opportunity for us to talk."

Adrianna fought a surge of disappointment. But to be

anything other than gracious about the change in plans would put Tripp—and Winn—in an awkward position.

"I'd love to dance with you." Adrianna smiled at Winn, then shifted her gaze to Tripp. "The one after that is yours."

Tripp leaned close and for one crazy second Adrianna thought he was going to kiss her. Instead he squeezed both her hands.

"The next and all the ones after that." Tripp gazed into her eyes, his tone brooking no argument.

"Absolutely." Adrianna felt as if she was floating. She wasn't sure what had happened to Tripp's normal hands-off behavior, but she was enjoying the change.

As Winn took her arm and led her to the dance floor, Adrianna felt Tripp's eyes on her. Hiding a smile, she added a little sway to her hips.

CHAPTER THREE

Tripp stood on the edge of the dance floor, schmoozing with a couple of donors, doing his best to ignore the music filling the ballroom. The romantic melody was almost as irritating as the cloying sweetness emanating from the large urn of fresh flowers positioned next to him.

He murmured words of agreement or occasionally nodded, enough to make the two men across from him believe they had his full attention. The truth was, conversing with them was merely a cover. It allowed Tripp to surreptitiously watch Adrianna while she danced with Winn.

The "important meeting" with Jim Ferris had taken just long enough for Winn to lead Adrianna to the dance floor. Tripp suspected the trustee's urgent need to talk had been merely a ploy to aid his son in getting what he wanted. Now, seeing the smirk on Winn's face as he held the brunette, Tripp was sure of it.

He wasn't surprised. Adrianna was a beautiful woman with a killer body, sculpted screen-goddess features and incredible green eyes.

The lithesome beauty seemed unaware of her appeal. She

always insisted she'd spent her childhood as somewhat of an ugly duckling and hadn't begun to blossom until college.

But Tripp had noticed her latent beauty back in high school. He'd made the mistake of mentioning his observation to Gayle. She'd gone ballistic.

That had been the first of many fights they'd had stemming from her irrational jealousy.

Even now, the simple act of appreciating the way Adrianna's dress emphasized her large breasts made him feel guilty. He lifted his gaze...and found her staring.

Not at Winn.

At *him.*

Tripp smiled back before refocusing his attention back on the donors.

Now, with his eyes elsewhere, he found himself thinking how much Adrianna's friendship had meant to him. Her supportive texts and emails following his wife's death had been a bright light during that dark period.

A comfortable closeness had developed over cyberspace. Even after the initial shock and grief had begun to subside, they'd continued to correspond, sharing thoughts and feelings they never would have shared in person.

It wasn't until Tripp returned to Jackson Hole that things turned awkward. He and Adrianna shared many of the same friends. Friends who'd recently begun marrying at alarming rates and who seemed to think they'd make a perfect match.

Now that he was home, the closeness they'd built somehow felt wrong now. He could almost hear Gayle sneering and telling him, "See, I was right. You *were* attracted to her." Which he knew wasn't the truth back then, but definitely was true now.

When Tripp had told his friends he was too busy to date, some assumed he was still grieving the loss of his wife and unborn daughter. Actually, Tripp was ready to move on. The irony was, now that he was ready, the one woman he was interested in was the one he couldn't bring himself to pursue. So he stuck with his original story that he didn't have time.

It was mostly the truth.

With declining Medicare reimbursement and pressure from insurance companies to accept deeper discounts, Tripp had to bring his A-game to work every day. If that weren't enough, his dad had been diagnosed with malignant melanoma.

See? Too busy.

Yet, he was grateful Adrianna had agreed to accompany him tonight. Especially because he and the beautiful brunette had achieved an understanding. They were simply friends with no expectations of more.

Tripp inhaled sharply as Winn slid his hand slowly up Adrianna's back. He narrowed his gaze. Anger surged. He'd made it clear to Winn that Adrianna was *his* date for the evening.

Actually, he'd taken it a step further. He'd let Winn believe Adrianna was his girlfriend. That was something he'd clear up later.

Once he pried Winn's hands off Adrianna's body.

The crowded dance floor could have explained why Winn held her so tightly, although Adrianna doubted that was the only reason. She guessed it had more to do with Tripp's unyielding gaze fixed on them and Winn's desire to jerk his chain.

She was certain Winn was aware of Tripp's scrutiny. Her "Tripp radar" had kicked in almost immediately upon reaching the dance floor. She'd waited until she was facing the right direction before slanting a quick glance where she'd last seen Tripp. Just as she'd thought, he was staring. Their eyes met and one look from his baby blues was all it took to send her pulse into overdrive.

Telling herself that it was supremely tacky to stare at one man while dancing with another, Adrianna pulled her gaze back to Winn.

"Being a midwife, I'm guessing you could find work anywhere." Halfway through the sentence his gaze dropped to her cleavage.

Adrianna waited, determined not to speak until he stopped conversing with her breasts.

Winn finally looked up. "With so many choices I'm surprised you ended up here."

It wasn't the first time she'd heard the ridiculous statement, but the sentiment always caught Adrianna off guard. As far as she was concerned, there wasn't a better place to live than surrounded by the majestic Tetons.

She gave a throaty laugh. "What's wrong with Jackson Hole?"

Winn's lips lifted in a lazy smile. "Well, for starters, it's a bit on the small side."

"That's part of its appeal." Adrianna loved seeing the babies she'd delivered when she went to the grocery store or stopped for a latte at Hill of Beans. "Besides, I grew up here. This is home."

A speculative look crossed Winn's face as he guided her across the dance floor, his movements fluid but not showy. "You and Tripp go way back."

Not as far back as Winn probably thought, but Adrianna wasn't about to admit that Tripp hadn't known she was alive back in high school. "We do."

"My father told me Tripp was married once but his wife died." The sympathy in Winn's eyes appeared sincere. While he came on a little strong, Adrianna had the feeling deep down Winn was a good guy. Too bad there was no spark.

"Gayle was a dear friend of mine." A familiar ache wrapped itself around Adrianna's heart. "A wonderful woman."

"I didn't realize you and she were friends." Winn lifted a brow. "Doesn't that make things awkward?"

"How do you mean?"

"Your friend was the one Tripp Randall chose to marry. Now she's gone and he turns to you." Winn's gaze fixed on her, gauging her reaction. "You don't deserve to be second best."

Adrianna instantly realized Winn had misconstrued her and Tripp's relationship. A little matter she could clear up with a few simple words. But it felt as though something more was going on here, something she couldn't put her finger on, something just beyond her reach.

She lifted her chin and gazed at him through lowered lashes. "If you knew me better, you'd know I'm not second best to anyone."

Winn's eyes turned hot and dark.

"I find confidence very sexy," he responded with a glittering smile. "I'm also a man who likes a challenge."

Adrianna cocked her head. "A challenge?"

"The way I see it, unless a woman has a wedding ring on her finger, she's available." As he spoke Winn slid one hand up her back.

Adrianna experienced a strange ticklish aversion to his touch. She was seized with a sudden urge to squirm...or slap his hand away.

"How close are you and Tripp Randall?" Winn asked in a low tone, his breath hot against her ear. "Is there the slightest possibility that another man—"

"I believe this is my dance."

Adrianna couldn't believe it when Tripp gently disengaged her from Winn's arms.

Strangely, Winn didn't protest.

"Thank you for the dance." Adrianna offered him a polite smile.

"It was a good beginning," Winn said, a twinkle in his eye. "I look forward to seeing you again and getting even better acquainted."

"What was that about?" Tripp took her in his arms. His

shoulder was hard beneath her hand, his arms steady as they began to dance.

"What do you mean?"

"Are you going to go out with him?" he asked, eyeing her.

Something about his tone rubbed Adrianna the wrong way. As much as she'd dreamed of more, she'd finally, reluctantly accepted that she and Tripp were just friends. After all, he'd made it clear friendship was all he wanted from her. Why was he acting as if she'd done something wrong by simply allowing another man to flirt with her?

You can't have it both ways, Tripp Randall.

"I may." She lifted a shoulder in a slight shrug. "If he asks."

Tripp's blue eyes darkened to black and his lips pressed together. "I don't trust him."

"You don't know him," Adrianna said mildly.

"You don't either," he shot back.

"Isn't that what dating is about...getting better acquainted?" Adrianna responded, instead of telling him that she had no interest in dating Winn Ferris.

"Doesn't it bother you that even though Winn believes we're dating, he continued to put some serious moves on you?" he murmured, twining a strand of her hair loosely around his fingers.

"Winn told me he considers any woman available as long as there's no wedding ring on her finger." Adrianna cursed herself for sounding breathless. But darn it, when the back of his knuckles brushed her cheek, it took everything she had not to close her eyes and sigh in ecstasy.

"Is that what you believe?" His voice gentled to a husky caress.

"No. Yes. I'm not sure." Adrianna found it hard to think clearly with him so near. "You and I aren't dating, so I don't see that it's any of your business who I see or don't see."

"I care about you, Adrianna." Tripp caught her hand in his,

lifted it to his mouth and pressed a kiss in the palm. Time seemed to stretch and extend as he looked deep into her eyes. "I'll find you a good man."

Her spine stiffened. She could feel it go hard vertebra by vertebra. She pushed away from him, irritation fueling her movements. The only problem she had in the man department was her attraction to Tripp, a man who didn't want to date her but apparently wanted to run her social life. "I don't mind your introducing me to your friends, but I'm more than capable of taking it from there."

Tripp made a scoffing sound. "You haven't been on a real date in months."

"That's not the point. I decided only last week to be more proactive on that front," Adrianna said with a studied nonchalance. "My dateless status will be changing soon."

Tripp's brows furrowed. "It's important not to move too fast."

The genuine concern in his voice and the protective look in his eyes whittled away at her irritation.

"I'm going to be thirty in less than a month." Adrianna experienced a pang at the thought. "If I want a husband and children, I need to get busy. Who knows—perhaps Winston Ferris will end up being my destiny?"

Tripp's arms tightened around her, bringing her closer. "He won't."

"I guess we're just going to have to see which one of us is right," she answered with a breezy sigh.

A soft expletive slipped past his lips. Tripp couldn't believe they were having this conversation. Winston Ferris was *not* Adrianna's destiny. Tripp knew that as well as he knew his own name.

As the sultry scent of Adrianna's perfume teased his nostrils and his gaze was drawn downward to her voluptuous breasts, he realized why he was so concerned.

Adrianna might give the appearance of being a woman of the

world, but it was all for show. He knew her secret. She was very much an innocent in the ways of men. Winn wasn't pursuing Adrianna with marriage in mind. The wealthy bachelor had a much simpler goal: get her into his bed.

"Tripp, I don't want to argue with you tonight." A self-conscious-sounding laugh escaped her lips.

His heart stumbled over itself at the worry reflected in the depths of her green eyes. "I don't want to argue with you either."

Determined to make this a wonderful evening for her, Tripp spent the rest of the dance and the ones that followed making sure Winn's name didn't come up. The conversation flowed effortlessly and Tripp was once again struck by how much he and Adrianna had in common.

After a fast-paced salsa that saw the older crowd exit the dance floor in droves, Adrianna mentioned she was thirsty. Taking her arm, he led them to one of the bars scattered around the large ballroom.

Because Adrianna was on call and couldn't drink, he got her a club soda and ordered himself a beer. After they'd gotten their drinks, they circled the ballroom. They were pushing their way through the densely packed crowd to say hello to some friends when they ran into Merle Bach, one of the trustees who'd been at their table for dinner.

Unfortunately, this time it wasn't Merle's wife at his side, but Jim Ferris.

"Good to see you both again." Merle favored them with a bright smile. With his snow-white hair, midsection paunch and jolly laugh, Merle had always reminded Tripp of Santa Claus...with cowboy boots. "I was telling Jim how much Helen and I enjoyed visiting with you and Adrianna. It's good to see you settling into the community."

"I grew up here, Merle." Tripp kept his tone light even as he tightened his hold on the bottle of beer. "It didn't take much for me to settle back in."

Tripp saw Merle and Jim exchange a quick, significant glance. It was common knowledge that when the previous hospital CEO had retired, Jim had liked another man for the position. The rumor was that while Jim conceded Tripp had the experience they needed, he hadn't liked the fact that Tripp was young and single.

"You know what I mean." Merle slapped him on the back and turned to Adrianna. "We couldn't be happier about the woman who's putting an end to your bachelor ways."

"You're a lucky man," Jim added.

Even though she stiffened beside him, Adrianna didn't say a word. Obviously she was leaving the delicate response to him.

Diplomacy and tact, Tripp told himself. He scrambled for the right words that wouldn't make Merle feel awkward for misunderstanding and also wouldn't be disrespectful to Adrianna.

"I've decided to have a barbecue at my place next Saturday," Jim announced before Tripp could respond. "A party to welcome my boy to Jackson Hole. I'll be inviting board members and many of the medical staff. I'm sure your parents will be there, Tripp. I hope we can also count on you and Adrianna."

Tripp hesitated. If he didn't take Adrianna, he knew who would. That would be tantamount to throwing her to the wolves.

He cared about her too much—er, she was too close a friend— for him to allow that to happen.

"I don't think I have anything on my calendar." Tripp slanted a sideways glance at Adrianna. "Do you remember if we had any plans?"

"No—" she cleared her throat "—I'm available."

"Well, I'm delighted you can make it," Jim said in a gravelly voice. "I know my son is disappointed that this lovely young woman is already taken, but I'm happy for you both."

Even though a polite smile remained on her lips, Adrianna gave Tripp a quick thrust of her elbow.

She was right. He needed to respond to Jim's statement, to make the limits of their "relationship" clear.

The words were poised on Tripp's lips when, out of the corner of his eye, he saw Winn approaching.

With an unsteady hand, Tripp slipped an arm around Adrianna's shoulders and smiled. "I feel lucky to have her in my life."

CHAPTER FOUR

Adrianna rocked slowly back and forth, smiling down at the baby cuddled in her arms. It was warm for early September, so she and Betsy had decided to sit outside on the front porch. The cottage in Jackson that Betsy and Ryan now called home had originally belonged to Betsy's great-aunt. After much renovation, it had a warm, homey feel that Adrianna's recently built condo could never hope to emulate.

She stared into baby Nathan's dark blue eyes and shared her most recent dilemma. "You remember Tripp. Yes, he's a nice guy. But we both know I was crazy for saying I'd go to the barbecue with him."

"I hate to tell you, but Nate's more concerned about his next meal than your social life." Betsy spoke through the screen door. She pushed it open and placed a tray filled with glasses of iced tea and a plate of snickerdoodle cookies on the small table. "You like Tripp. Why not go to a party with him?"

Betsy settled herself into a matching rocker, apparently content to leave the baby in Adrianna's arms.

"I want what you have, Bets." Adrianna lifted the crystal tumbler with one hand, careful not to disturb the infant in her arms. "How am I going to find Mr. Right if I keep hanging out with Tripp?"

Instead of tossing out some platitude, her friend's expression turned thoughtful. "I understand. I really do. But it's obvious Tripp likes you. Perhaps, given time—"

"He's not going to come around." Adrianna spoke so loudly the baby stirred in her arms. She softened her tone. "Tripp has made it perfectly clear that he thinks of me only as a friend."

"At the country club he was being so attentive—"

"A dog with his bone. Nothing more." Although the realization hurt, Adrianna refused to sugarcoat the truth. "Winn was showing interest. Tripp reacted."

"If you're so convinced there's no hope, why are you going with him to the party?"

Exactly the question Adrianna had been asking herself.

"Well, Winn will be there." Adrianna settled back against the rocker and tried to picture the dark-haired man. Unfortunately, the only male image that sprang to mind had blond hair and cheek stubble. She determinedly blinked it away. "It'll give me the opportunity to get to know him without going on an actual date."

"I guess that *could* occur." Betsy chewed on her lower lip, her gaze thoughtful. "Unless Tripp continues to play the possessive-boyfriend card."

That was definitely a possibility. Adrianna sighed. Perhaps she should cancel. Of course, with the party scheduled for tomorrow night, if she was going to bail on Tripp, she had to tell him soon. She rubbed the bridge of her nose. "Maybe I should forget about men, get a couple cats and save myself all this stress."

"Yeah, right," Betsy said with a laugh.

Adrianna had done so much thinking about her situation that her head felt ready to explode. "Enough about me. What's new with you? Other than having a wonderful husband and this fabulous baby boy."

"Well..." Betsy stared at the tea in her hands. She cleared her throat, then lifted her gaze. "Keenan may be getting a new trial."

Adrianna had known Betsy's older brother since childhood. Keenan McGregor had been a fearless risk taker, brilliant but angry. Angry at his mother for being a drunk, angry at watching his little sister go without food, angry at the lousy cards he'd been dealt in life.

Still, as volatile as Keenan had been, Adrianna believed—as Betsy did—that he was innocent of the crime that had sent him to the penitentiary in Rawlins two years ago.

"That's wonderful news," Adrianna said cautiously, knowing that it would be an uphill battle for someone already convicted to get a new trial. "Is his public defender spearheading the effort?"

"As if that would ever happen," Betsy snorted, a look of disgust on her face. "No, Keenan has finally agreed to let Cole and Ryan help him. You know how resistant my brother has been about accepting assistance from family or friends."

"I remember." Betsy had been devastated when Keenan had refused to take her savings to hire a better attorney when he was originally brought up on charges. "What changed?"

"I don't want to say he found religion—that's a bit too clichéd." Betsy's lips twisted in a wry smile. "But one of the prison chaplains somehow convinced him there's no shame in accepting assistance."

"I'm so glad." Adrianna reached over and squeezed her friend's hand.

"Ryan is now in charge of the legal team. Cole insisted on hiring—and paying for—a private investigator."

Cole Lassiter had also been Keenan's friend growing up. He'd come from a similar home situation as Betsy and Keenan, but had turned his frustration into determination and now was the head of Hill of Beans, with over twenty-five coffee shops west of the Mississippi, including one in Jackson Hole.

"Have they unearthed any new evidence?" Adrianna asked.

"It's looking that way," Betsy said cautiously. "I'm trying not to get my hopes up."

"I'll say a little prayer for him."

"I'd appreciate it." A truck turned the corner and Betsy gave Adrianna a curious look. "Have you decided what you're going to do about Tripp?"

"You mean since we last spoke about him a minute ago?" Adrianna's lips twisted upward. "I still have time to make up my mind."

The barbecue wasn't until tomorrow night. Once she left Betsy's house, Adrianna had a full schedule of appointments at the clinic where she practiced with two female ob-gyns. After her last appointment, she planned to do a pro–con list and then make her decision. If she decided to opt out, that would still give Tripp twenty-four hours to find someone else.

Even though she told herself she didn't care, the thought of Tripp attending the party with another woman made Adrianna reach for a cookie. And she didn't even like snickerdoodles.

"I'd say you have about sixty seconds."

Confused, Adrianna followed her friend's gaze to the street where two men were getting out of a pickup.

Her traitorous heart skipped a beat. When Tripp saw her and lifted a hand, she had little choice but to smile and wave.

"What's he doing here?" she asked Betsy, keeping the smile firmly on her lips.

"No idea." Betsy rose to her feet. "Ryan called earlier and said he'd be stopping by to pick up the laptop he'd forgotten. He didn't mention bringing Tripp with him."

Of course he didn't, Adrianna thought with a sigh.

She glanced down at her stylish paisley dress and heels. At least she looked presentable. Not that it mattered. After all, Tripp was just a friend.

Betsy greeted her husband on the steps to the porch, wrapping her arms around his neck and ardently kissing him.

Inside the house, a Pomeranian barked a welcome.

"Maybe we should have someone around to hold the baby more often." Ryan stepped back with obvious reluctance, keeping his arm around his wife's shoulders.

"Looking good, Betsy." Tripp's words made the new mom blush.

Adrianna knew the compliment was sincere. Even though Betsy often referred to herself as a "Plain Jane," nothing could be further from the truth. Her friend looked adorable in a flirty blue print skirt and cotton sweater.

Tripp shifted his gaze to Adrianna. "You look lovely, too, Ms. Lee."

"As do you, Mr. Randall." Actually, Tripp looked positively yummy in a dark suit and gray shirt. As he stepped close, Adrianna discovered he smelled just as good as he looked. A thousand times more appetizing than the cookie in her hand. Adrianna dropped it to her plate and cocked her head. "Isn't this a workday for you?"

"I might ask you the same question," he responded with a raised brow.

"It's my morning off," she informed him. "I have clinic this afternoon."

"I'm taking an early lunch," Tripp explained.

She smiled. "Pays to be the boss."

Out of the corner of her eye, Adrianna saw that Ryan had pulled Betsy close once again. They were speaking so softly she couldn't hear what they were saying.

"He seems to be a good baby." Tripp crouched down beside Adrianna, a curved finger caressing the baby's soft cheek.

His gaze took on a distant look and Adrianna wondered if he was thinking of the baby he'd lost. Her heart clenched. Sometimes life simply wasn't fair.

"I confirmed the barbecue tomorrow night starts at seven."

Tripp's blue eyes met hers. "I thought I'd pick you up around six-thirty?"

Something has come up and I'm not able to make it after all. The words, poised on the tip of her tongue, morphed as they hit her lips.

"Sounds good," she heard herself say. *Nonono.* "I mean—"

"Tripp—" Ryan motioned to him "—do you have a second to look at the notes on Keenan's case?"

"You're in on the effort to get Keenan released?" Adrianna didn't know why she was so surprised. Tripp had been part of that close-knit group of athletes and friends.

"Not yet." Tripp pulled to his feet. "But when I heard what was going on, I told Ryan I wanted to help."

Tell him you can't go with him to the party, Adrianna's inner voice nagged. Tell him now.

"I—"

Before she could get another word out, Tripp smiled at her. "I'm really looking forward to tomorrow night."

"You are?" Sounding like a frog was definitely not Adrianna's style. She cleared her throat, prepared to try again.

"Tripp," Ryan called out, "I have a client coming at two, so I don't have long."

"Coming." But before Tripp headed into the house, he surprised Adrianna by reaching over and squeezing her shoulder. "See you tomorrow."

"I'll be ready," Adrianna murmured.

The flash of his smile sent desire coursing through her veins like honey and red flags popping up.

When the screen door closed behind the two men, Betsy turned to Adrianna. "Sounds like you made your decision."

"It appears so."

Yes, she'd made a decision. The trouble was, Adrianna was gripped with the sinking feeling it was the wrong one.

When Adrianna opened her front door the next day and saw Tripp wearing jeans and a twill shirt that made his eyes look extra blue, her heart skipped a beat. She tried to ignore the flutter as she motioned him inside.

Although Adrianna rarely wore denim, for a Jackson Hole outdoor barbecue she'd made an exception. She'd coupled her skinny jeans with a double V-neck lattice-back top in a rich emerald-green.

After glancing longingly at the stilettos in her closet, she'd settled for a pair of kitten heels. Walking over uneven terrain made anything over an inch impractical.

"I've never seen someone look so pretty in denim," Tripp said, his gaze lingering on the tight-fitting jeans.

Adrianna couldn't help herself. A shiver raced up her spine. "I could say the same about you."

"Pretty? Good Gawd, I hope not." Tripp laughed aloud, then grinned. "I can never predict what's going to come out of your mouth, Ms. Lee."

"It'd be boring if you could," she said with a wink.

They walked to Tripp's truck side by side but not touching. Which was exactly what she wanted Adrianna told herself.

Tripp pulled the door open for her and Adrianna climbed into the vehicle without assistance. The way he made her feel, the less they touched the better.

"Do you know who's going to be at this event?" she asked after he'd slid behind the wheel and the truck pulled away from the curb. "Will there be anyone we know?"

We know. Sheesh. Adrianna flushed. Anyone hearing her would think they were a couple. Which was not how she meant it at all. Thankfully, Tripp's lack of reaction told her he hadn't noticed her faux pas.

His brow furrowed in thought. "I believe Nick Delacourt told me he and Lexi were coming. If I had to guess, I'd say David and July Wahl will be there, too."

Nick was a prominent family law attorney, who divided his time between his Dallas practice and the one he'd started in Jackson Hole. He'd met and married social worker Lexi several years ago after he was forced to remain in Jackson Hole while recovering from a serious skiing accident.

Hospital Chief of Staff Dr. David Wahl and his photographer wife, July, were also part of the wide circle of friends that Adrianna and Tripp shared. Of course, even after only a year of being back in Jackson Hole, Tripp was more firmly ensconced in the group than she would ever be. As Adrianna often told her good friend Betsy, she didn't do groups well. Actually, she wasn't that great one-on-one either.

"I wonder if Winn will be here tonight," Adrianna mused when they turned off the highway onto the long, black-topped lane leading to the house.

Tripp slanted a sideways glance in her direction. "Do you want him to be?"

Adrianna lifted one shoulder in a slight shrug and answered honestly. "I'm not sure. I don't feel any particular chemistry with him, but then, we just met."

Tripp's lips tightened. "I take it you're still on your manhunt?"

The tone of his voice made it clear he didn't approve. She told herself she didn't care. What she did wasn't any of his business.

"I wouldn't put it quite that way, but yes, I'm hoping to find someone special." Adrianna refused to apologize for wanting a special man in her life. "Do you like coming home to an empty house?"

"Not particularly," he said quietly. "But my life is so busy right now I don't have time for a relationship."

We make time for what's important. The words were on the tip of her tongue but Adrianna pulled them back. It was obvious to her—and to other friends—that Tripp and Gayle's relationship had been a special one and that he was having difficulty moving on.

Strangely, knowing that no woman would likely ever measure up to what Tripp had shared with Gayle made his disinterest in her slightly more palatable.

"I'm sure it's hard," Adrianna acknowledged. "When you've had the best, it'd be hard to settle for less."

Tripp acted as if he hadn't heard her, opening his door and rounding the front of the truck to reach her. When she stepped out, he was waiting.

"Jim Ferris thinks you and I are together," he said in a conversational tone as they started up the walk.

"You mean he knows you're bringing me to party."

"No," Tripp continued in the same nonchalant tone as they approached the sprawling log structure, "Jim thinks you're my girlfriend."

Confused, Adrianna turned to him. "Because we danced together at the country club?"

"That, and the fact that we'd come to that event together." Tripp raked a hand through his hair. "I should have said something then, cleared up the misunderstanding."

"Why didn't you?"

"I don't know. Maybe I didn't want to make him look like a fool for making such an assumption. Maybe I didn't want to piss him off." Tripp paused at the foot of the wooden steps leading to the home's front porch. "Did you know that Jim tried to block my appointment? He didn't like it that I was single. He wanted a family guy for the position."

"You have fabulous credentials," Adrianna sputtered. "I read all the bios when the *Jackson Hole News* reported on the candidates. You were far and away the most qualified."

Tripp smiled at her vehemence. "Remember, they did pick me."

"They would have been stupid if they hadn't," Adrianna

retorted, then paused. "But you were selected, so why does it matter what Ferris thinks about your single status?"

"It doesn't. I'll make sure he understands tonight that you and I are simply friends," Tripp said apologetically. "If you'd like, I'll also make it clear to Winn that you're available."

Adrianna waved a dismissive hand. "Not necessary."

Tripp's gaze searched her face. "Are you sure?"

Adrianna offered him a reassuring smile. "I believe that for Winn my perceived unavailability is part of my appeal."

"But if he thinks you're with me, he won't—"

"I'm sure his father will eventually tell him the news."

"That might not be right away."

Even though part of her reason for coming was to check out Winn as a potential future date, Adrianna found this sudden need of Tripp to matchmake extremely irritating. She fisted her hands on her hips and narrowed her eyes. "Were you hoping to pawn me off on Winn tonight?"

"Absolutely not," he said, looking properly horrified.

"Well, then, you're stuck with me," she said, somewhat mollified. "At least for tonight."

"Excellent." Tripp flashed a wolfish grin and rang the bell.

Adrianna was still mulling over that response when Jim Ferris opened the door. The older man's broad smile included them both.

"Welcome." He motioned them inside. "Everyone is out back. Let me show you the way."

Tripp and Jim engaged in small talk while Adrianna was content to walk beside them and admire the interior of the ranch home with its open-beamed ceilings and elegant understated casualness.

"Adrianna." She heard Lexi's voice ring out a welcome the second they stepped onto the back patio.

She turned and saw the pretty brunette and another good

friend, July Wahl, standing next to a large urn of multicolored mums.

Adrianna lightly touched Tripp's arm, distracting him from his conversation with Jim.

"If you need me, I'll be over chatting with July and Lexi." She gestured with her head toward the two women.

"Jim wants to introduce me to a couple of guys, then I'll join you," Tripp assured her.

"No worries." Adrianna smiled up at him. "I'll be fine."

As she walked away she heard Jim murmur something about how lucky he was to be with someone so understanding. She didn't hear Tripp's reply but it scarcely mattered.

Adrianna wasn't with Tripp.

He knew it.

She knew it.

As soon as Tripp had a chance to tell him, Jim Ferris would know it, too.

CHAPTER FIVE

"I love your shirt," July gushed when Adrianna drew close. "The color makes your eyes look incredibly green."

"I like yours, too." Adrianna recognized the striped Galao pullover from the Anthropologie catalog. She shifted her gaze to Lexi. As expected, the social worker known for her fashion acumen had eschewed denim and worn khakis, pairing the tan-colored pants with a black scalloped lace top. "You look gorgeous as ever, Mrs. Delacourt."

Lexi rolled her eyes. "Thank you, *Ms. Lee.* I think we all look pretty hot this evening."

"I'd say we're easily the sexiest women here," July drawled.

"That's because we're the only women here under sixty," Adrianna said with a little laugh.

"True." Lexi grinned and took a sip of what looked like a margarita on the rocks, salt encircling the rim of the glass.

Adrianna gazed at the drink. "What is that?"

"A Crazy Coyote Margarita," July answered first. "I just finished one. Very tasty."

"They're certainly not skimping on the alcohol." Lexi made a face. "Oh, my, this could go straight to my head."

"Lightweight," July teased. "Seemed fine to me."

"What's the difference between that and a regular margarita?" Adrianna asked, willing to admit her ignorance. She'd never been much of a drinker.

"I had the same question," July admitted. "The bartender said they use Coyote Gold margarita mix, which tells me absolutely nothing."

"May I get you something to drink?" A young man dressed in black and obviously part of the catering staff stopped beside her.

"I'll have a Crazy Coyote Margarita," Adrianna told him.

"Good choice," July said approvingly.

Lexi took another sip, her lips twisting slightly upward. "If you want to live dangerously."

Adrianna thought about telling Lexi she already was...by being here with Tripp.

"You and Tripp came together," Lexi said as if she'd read her mind. Her friend was trying to act casual, but the spark of interest in her eyes gave her away.

"As friends only." Adrianna's gaze drifted to the fire pit where a hog lay skewered on a rotisserie spit, roasting as it rotated. She grimaced and quickly pulled her gaze away. "I think I'm going to become a vegetarian."

July's sea-green eyes lit with interest. "Seriously? Since when?"

"Since she saw the hog over there, you goof." Lexi smiled good-naturedly, but the look in her eyes said she wasn't fooled by the abrupt change in conversation.

July didn't even look in the direction of the fire pit. Instead she turned her body toward Adrianna just as the young man from the catering company returned with her drink order.

"Here you go, ma'am." He handed the chilled glass edged in salt to her with a flourish. "One Crazy Coyote Margarita."

"Ah, thank you." Adrianna closed her fingers around the glass. She waited until the college-aged boy was out of earshot before she turned to her friends. "Did you hear that? He called me 'ma'am.'"

"Well, you are almost thirty." Lexi managed to keep a remarkably straight face. "That's when the downward slide begins. Isn't that right, July?"

"Speak for yourself, Lex." July offered up an impish smile. "I haven't hit that milestone yet."

"What milestone?"

Tripp must have sneaked up while they were talking because he now stood beside her.

"The big three-zero." July glanced pointedly in her direction. "The catering guy called Adrianna 'ma'am.'"

Tripp looked surprised. "Did you recently turn thirty?"

He doesn't even know my birthday. The fact illustrated just how little they were connected. A pang stabbed Adrianna's heart and she took a sip of her drink, immediately noticing Lexi had been right. The bartender was being *very* generous with the tequila.

"I'll turn thirty at the end of the month," Adrianna informed Tripp when she realized he was waiting for a reply. "September 28. Mark it on your calendar."

The ridiculousness of her response caused Adrianna to take another drink. Tripp didn't care when her birthday was; he'd only asked to be polite. And she doubted he'd be keeping track.

"I've made a mental note of it," he said.

"Made a mental note of what?" Winn sauntered up, a bottle of beer hanging loosely from his fingers.

"Adrianna's birthday," July informed him.

Winn's eyes widened in surprise. His disbelieving gaze settled on Tripp. "You didn't know your girlfriend's birthday?"

"She's not—" July began but stopped when Lexi elbowed her.

"I knew it was at the end of this month." Tripp shrugged. "I wasn't sure of the exact date."

A smile tugged at Winn's lips as he shook his head. "No excuse."

Adrianna drained her glass like a college student on spring break. Considering she had very little in her stomach, it wasn't a smart move. Of course, neither was falling in love with a man who didn't want her. For some odd reason, at the moment, the thought seemed more amusing than sad. Adrianna smiled. "I agree with you, Winn."

Surprise filled Winn's eyes. "You do?"

"I bet you're not the kind of man to forget a woman's birthday." Feeling uncharacteristically reckless, Adrianna slipped her hand around his arm and gazed up at him, batting her heavily mascaraed lashes.

"If you're asking if I'd ever forget your birthday," Winn said gallantly, "the answer is no."

Adrianna let her gaze linger. Winn Ferris was a handsome man. His white shirt was the perfect foil for his dark hair. Even dressed simply in black jeans and a white shirt, he managed to look...elegant.

"Would you like another Crazy Coyote, ma'am?" The boy—er, waiter—asked, taking her empty glass.

Even though common sense told Adrianna to wait until she'd eaten before imbibing more alcohol, she wasn't on call this weekend and Tripp was driving.

Winn glanced at her and smiled.

It was all the encouragement she needed. "I'd love another."

"Do you think that's wise, Adrianna?" Tripp's voice sounded in her ear.

"She's a big girl, Randall." Winn patted her hand in a proprietary gesture. "I'm sure she can make up her own mind."

"Adrianna," Tripp said softly but with a degree of urgency.

She met his gaze. As his baby blues sucked her in she saw confusion and something that startled her. The man who didn't know her birthday appeared to be genuinely worried. About *her*.

Adrianna wished she could tell Tripp that he needn't be

concerned. Though she'd been blinded by a handsome face in college, she was older now. And hopefully wiser.

"There's someone I'd like you to meet." Tripp's gaze never left her face. "If you have a moment."

"I think—" Winn began, but Adrianna surprised herself by closing his lips with her fingers.

"I need to go." She slipped her hand out from around Winn's arm and turned toward Tripp. "I love meeting new people."

"Since when?" July muttered and Lexi shushed her.

With a relieved smile Tripp took her arm. She strolled across the patio with him, swearing she could smell a hint of fall in the warm night air. When he pulled her around the corner of the house and stopped, Adrianna glanced around. They were alone. "Who did you want me to meet?"

He gently tucked a strand of hair behind her ear. "Me."

The tequila must have affected Adrianna more than she'd realized because what he said made no sense. "Pardon?"

"I wanted you to be with me, not Winn." His gaze searched hers. "Are you angry?"

Adrianna pushed her hair back from her face with the back of her hand. "Not angry," she admitted. "Confused."

"Why confused?" He gave his head a slight shake when the waiter rounded the corner of the house, margarita in hand. The young man immediately turned on his heel.

"We both know you don't want me." Then because that sounded so plaintive, she added, "Of course I don't want you either. Other than as a friend, of course."

"Of course," he murmured.

Now, Winn was another story. The look in his eyes said he wanted to be a whole lot more than friends.

A sudden thought hit her. "Does Jim Ferris now know that you and I are simply friends?"

That would certainly explain why Winn was being so bold, causing Tripp to overreact.

Tripp shook his head. "I haven't had the chance to speak privately with him yet. I will," he hastily added.

"Make sure you do." Adrianna wasn't sure what kind of game Tripp was playing. She just knew it was time for it to come to an end. "Tonight."

～

Tripp was surprised to see his parents walk through the door just as everyone was sitting down to eat. He'd been over to see his dad earlier in the day, but the older man hadn't been feeling well and his mother thought they might skip the barbecue.

Even though his last round of chemo had been almost a month ago, the family was still waiting for him to bounce back. Tonight his dad actually looked...better. Certainly he looked better than he had last week and much better than he had this morning.

He and Adrianna had been about to join their friends at one of the many tables set up for the event. When Tripp saw his parents, he touched Adrianna's arm. "My parents just arrived."

"Oh." She inclined her head. "Shall we sit with them?"

Tripp searched her eyes to make sure the offer was sincere. Because he'd come with Adrianna, his first loyalty was to her. But he knew how much it would mean for his parents to share the meal with them. "You don't mind?"

"Not at all." Adrianna turned toward their friends. "Tripp's folks decided to come after all, and we promised to sit with them."

As expected, their friends understood.

Tripp's mother's face lit up when she saw them approach. His father's lips lifted in a slow smile.

"You look pretty this evening," his dad said to Adrianna.

"Thank you, Mr. Randall," Adrianna said, blushing prettily.

Frank lifted a brow. "Are we going to have to go through this each time we see each other?"

"Frank," Adrianna said. "How nice to see you again."

Tripp cast a sideways glance at his mother and found her watching the exchange, a tremulous smile on her lips.

"I wasn't sure you'd be here," his mother said to him. "I know Jim Ferris isn't one of your favorite people—"

"Kathy." His father spoke sharply, though in an equally low tone. "Jim is our host."

His mother's cheeks turned a bright pink and an uncomfortable silence descended over the foursome.

"I see a table for four over there," Adrianna said.

"Are you inviting us to eat with you?" his mother asked, obviously not wanting to read anything into her comment.

"Only if you want to," Adrianna said quickly.

"Yes, Mother," Tripp said, almost at the same time. "We'd like you and Dad to eat with us."

"Offer accepted." His father sounded almost jovial. "It'll give me a chance to get to know this little lady better."

His dad smiled warmly at Adrianna and Tripp realized he must make it clear to his parents that he and the pretty midwife were just friends. But that discussion could wait.

He wanted them to enjoy the evening. And he didn't feel like answering their questions as to why he wasn't interested in Adrianna.

Conversation flowed easily over dinner and for a normally shy person, Adrianna talked a great deal. Although his parents were very adept in social settings, his suspicions were that Adrianna's talkativeness had more to do with a second Crazy Coyote Margarita that the waiter brought her than his parents' natural friendliness.

His mother continued to smile warmly at Adrianna, which worried Tripp. She'd been doing that all through dinner. The two women had bonded over their inability to eat anything cooked with an intact face.

Then she'd asked Adrianna about her work. His mother's eyes shone when Adrianna had gushed about how much she loved delivering babies.

When his mother lifted a brow and a gleam filled her eye, Tripp shifted uneasily in his seat.

"I assume you want children of your own?" his mother asked.

"I do," Adrianna said without hesitation. "But I'd like to find a husband first."

When his mother's gaze slid pointedly to him, Tripp realized he should have seen it coming.

He ignored the look she shot him and stabbed the last piece of pork on his plate. "Did I tell you that our emergency department received another honor?"

"Honey—" his mom's tone turned chiding "—can't you forget about work for one evening?"

He resisted the urge to point out that she and Adrianna had been talking about her "work" for the past ten minutes.

"Your mother is right."

Tripp couldn't believe his father was agreeing with his mom. Frank had been a businessman as well as a rancher for most of his life. He understood that events such as tonight's barbecue were as much about business as socializing.

"We appreciate the fact that you're encouraging Tripp to get out more," Frank said to Adrianna.

Whoa, what had his father said? Tripp had been the one to invite Adrianna to this event, not the other way around.

"He can be somewhat of a workaholic." Adrianna cast him a teasing glance and motioned for the server to bring her another Crazy Coyote.

"Are those good?" his mother asked.

"Delicious," Adrianna pronounced.

"I'll have one, too," his mother told the server.

Tripp resisted the urge to groan.

His father settled back in his chair, looking amused. "You enjoy being with my son."

"I do." Adrianna focused on his dad, her green eyes glowing. "Tripp, well, you just never know what's going to come out of his mouth."

"What?" Tripp sputtered.

"Oh, honey—" his mother patted his arms "—she's teasing you."

The server returned far too quickly with drinks for his mother and Adrianna. Tripp wondered if the guy would take a bribe not to come around again.

"Look at that full moon," his father said.

Tripp stared at his dad. Talking about the *moon?* Had his dad been drinking, too?

"A beautiful night for a walk." His mother gave a decisive nod. "Don't you agree?"

When his father didn't respond, Tripp stepped in. It would be good for his parents to take a short walk. "I agree."

"You and Adrianna must take advantage of it."

Tripp stared unblinking at his dad even as he realized he'd walked right into that one and had only himself to blame. His father's hopeful expression made it difficult to deny him anything. Even a walk in the moonlight with a woman he considered only a friend.

"Perhaps Adrianna isn't into walking." Tripp scrambled for an excuse. "She's wearing heels."

"Pssh. Kitten ones." Adrianna rose to her feet and stretched, her top pulling tight against her breasts. "I could run a marathon in these."

She reached over and picked up her half-finished margarita glass.

Tripp plucked it from her fingers and placed it back on the table.

She cocked her head.

He held out his hand. "Ready?"

She smiled and something in his heart stirred. He told himself it was only because she was so beautiful. Any man would be likewise affected.

Adrianna placed her hand in his and they strolled toward the back of the property. He forced himself to drop her hand when they stopped on the way to speak with a couple of members of the board of trustees. Thankfully, Adrianna's alcohol intake didn't seem to impair her ability to converse intelligently.

Still, he was relieved when they left the guests behind and made their way to a split-rail fence overlooking a meadow. The moon cast a golden glow over the ranchland stretched out before them as far as the eye could see.

Placing her arms on the upper rail, Adrianna leaned forward and sighed. "I love Jackson Hole. I don't know why anyone ever leaves here."

"We both left," Tripp pointed out. "If we wanted to attend college, we had to go."

Leaving Wyoming to get his bachelor's and then his master's degree had been a necessity. The experience Tripp had gained working in New York City had been vital to his getting his current position. Yet, Adrianna was right. During all those years away, he'd never stopped missing Jackson Hole.

"You stayed away a long time," he heard her say.

"Too long." Tripp stared into the darkness, remembering all the years he'd tried to persuade Gayle they should return. "We think our parents are going to live forever."

"Nothing in life is guaranteed," she said with a heavy sigh, then appeared to shrug off her melancholy and smiled. "Your father looks good tonight. How is he doing?"

"We're waiting to see how his body has responded to this latest round of chemotherapy." Tripp cleared his throat. "I'm...hopeful."

Adrianna surprised him by stroking his arm. "I have a good feeling."

Dear God, he hoped her feeling was borne out in the upcoming lab tests. He loved his father. The thought of losing him...

Emotion welled up inside Tripp. He couldn't think of losing him. Couldn't talk about losing him. "You smell good."

"Verbena and lavender," Adrianna informed him, not mentioning the abrupt change in subject."

"Very nice."

"I'm glad you like it," she said in a husky voice that reminded him of tangled sheets and entwined legs. The sounds of the party faded and the darkness closed in around them.

Adrianna took a step forward. Or had he moved closer?

Regardless, it seemed so natural to wrap his arms around her and pull her to him. Her curves molded to his body perfectly.

Her fingers played with his hair. "Did I ever tell you how much I like these little waves just above your collar?"

"I don't believe so." He nuzzled her ear. "Have I told you I like the way you smell?"

She giggled and he didn't know who was more surprised. He never thought he'd hear Adrianna Lee *giggle.*

"What's so funny?" He slid his hand up her spine.

"Not five seconds ago you told me you liked my lotion."

He paused, then chuckled. "You're right. I don't know what I was thinking."

She lifted a finger and pressed it against his lips. "You were thinking about kissing me."

"I was?"

She nodded. "Yep."

Giggling. Saying *yep.* The woman had obviously had too much to drink.

"Want to know how I know that?"

"Sure."

"Because I'm thinking the same thing."

"You want to kiss me?"

She nodded, her eyes glittering. "You're super sexy."

"You've had too much to drink."

"I had two margaritas." She cocked her head and brought a finger to her lips. "Or was it three?"

"And very little to eat."

"Why, Mr. Randall, have you been spying on me?" she said in mock outrage before another giggle escaped her lips.

Okay, it was official. Adrianna was buzzed. Which meant only a cad would take advantage of a woman in her condition.

Tripp didn't bother to examine the disappointment coursing through him. Stepping back, he took her arm. "We should get back."

She dug in her kitten heels and lifted her chin. "I'm not going anywhere until you kiss me."

Her eyes were large and luminous. It took every ounce of strength Tripp possessed to not pull her into his arms and give her what she was asking for. What she wanted. What *he* wanted.

The realization surprised him. While Adrianna was a beautiful woman—that fact would be impossible for any red-blooded male to deny—he'd never seen her as anything more than Gayle's friend. The idea that he would even seriously consider kissing her was mildly disturbing.

Yet when she unexpectedly wrapped her arms around him and pressed her lips firmly against his, Tripp could only react.

Unfortunately—er, *fortunately*—the kiss was over almost as soon as it had begun.

"What was that about?" he heard himself say.

She shrugged. "I guess I wanted to see what kissing you would be like."

"I was an experiment?"

"Don't look at me like that." Adrianna gave a little laugh. "It was okay. Not great, but good."

Before he could respond, she shifted her gaze toward the house. "You're right. We better get back."

Without another word, she started off on a brisk trot in the direction of the party. He had to hustle to keep up.

As he watched her cute little derriere swing from side to side, he couldn't help feeling like an Olympic contender who'd been cut out of the medals.

His kiss had been only good.

Not great.

CHAPTER SIX

Because Adrianna had Sunday off, she slept in. Last night when she'd gone to bed she thought about setting her alarm so she could make it to church, but one too many Crazy Coyote Margaritas swayed the vote.

By the time she pushed back her quilt, ready to face the day, it was almost ten. After popping a couple of aspirins, she found herself humming as she showered and dressed for a relaxing day at home in black leggings and a garnet-colored cotton shirt. It wasn't until she drank from a carton of orange juice and felt the cool tang against her lips that a memory from last night surfaced.

She'd kissed Tripp.

What was I thinking?

She hadn't been thinking. That was the problem. Hadn't she learned from the past? From that horrible senior year in college? A person had to be alert at all times. The alcohol had been a mistake.

Deep down she knew the kiss had more to do with the way Tripp made her feel, rather than any alcohol she'd consumed. The Crazy Coyotes had merely let the barriers she normally kept in place slip.

The ring of her cell phone jarred her from her reverie. Even though she wasn't on call, if one of her patients presented ready to deliver, she would be notified.

She hurried across the room and snatched her phone from the counter. "Adrianna Lee."

"Adrianna," a pleasant feminine voice responded, "this is Kathy. I hope I didn't wake you."

"Kathy?" Her muddled brain fumbled for a connection.

"Tripp's mother," the woman said with a laugh in her voice.

"Of course. Mrs. Randall, how are you?"

"I'm very well, thank you. And it's Kathy, not Mrs. Randall." There was a slight pause before she continued. "I wondered if you had lunch plans."

"Uh, no, I don't."

"Wonderful. Would you be interested in meeting me at the Green Gâteau?"

The small bistro on Scott Lane was one of Adrianna's favorite places to dine.

"I'd love to," Adrianna said, then paused. "Will Tripp be joining us?"

"No." Kathy's tone remained light. "Just the two of us. Will noon work?"

"That will be perfect."

On the drive to the bistro, Adrianna almost wished it had been the hospital calling. At least she'd know what to expect. She hadn't a clue why Tripp's mother wanted to have lunch with her.

At five minutes before twelve Adrianna walked through the door of the quaint bistro that was a favorite of the women in Jackson Hole. With an eclectic atmosphere that included stained glass, tin ceilings and mismatched pub chairs and tables, the place had a funky but homey feel.

Kathy motioned to her from a small table by the window. Looking stylish as always in a wrap dress in muted celery-green and a light cotton sweater, her appearance made Adrianna glad she'd changed into a pair of linen pants.

When she reached the table, Kathy stood and greeted Adrianna with a hug. "I'm happy you could make it."

"Thanks for inviting me," Adrianna murmured, settling into the chair across the table. "You look nice today. I love that color on you."

"Oh, my dear, you're the one who's drawing everyone's eyes."

Adrianna didn't bother to glance around. She'd learned long ago that men simply liked to check out women. That didn't mean they were interested in dating them. Her never-ending dateless status was proof of that fact.

They chatted about the weather for several minutes, then ordered the special: a vegetable quiche with a side of fruit and mango iced tea. After the waitress had brought their beverages, Kathy's expression turned serious.

Her gaze searched Adrianna's face. "I suppose you're wondering why I asked you to meet me today."

Adrianna took a sip of tea and let a smile be her answer.

"You know Frank has cancer." A bleak look filled the older woman's eyes. "While we're hopeful he'll have a good response to this latest round of chemo, he's very ill."

Adrianna reached across the table and impulsively squeezed the woman's hand.

"Seeing Tripp settling down has made Frank very happy."

Adrianna started to nod. Then it hit her. Settling down? Something was very wrong here.

"It was hard on everyone when Gayle and the baby died." Kathy stared down at the cloth napkin in her lap for several long seconds before lifting her gaze. "Tripp was inconsolable."

"He loved her very much."

Kathy nodded. "I believe Gayle wouldn't have wanted him to grieve forever. She'd have wanted him to move on."

Adrianna couldn't argue with that. "He has to be ready."

"I believe he finally is."

"I'm not so sure," Adrianna murmured.

"Oh, he's ready." A pleased smile tugged at his mother's coral lips. "Everyone at the party was commenting how he couldn't take his eyes off you."

She wondered what Tripp's mother would say if she told her the real reason she was there with her son.

"Even though getting together today might seem to indicate otherwise, I want to assure you that I'll never be a meddling mother-in-law."

"But Tripp and I—"

Kathy waved her silent.

"Please, let me finish. We don't know how much time Frank has left, but it would make both of us extremely happy to see Tripp married before..." Kathy swallowed hard. "I'm just saying Frank would love to see his son settled down with you."

"Kathy, I—" Adrianna had been prepared to tell his mother everything. How she and Tripp were simply friends. How he'd invited her to go with him to the event at the country club so they'd both be free to network. How Jim Ferris had misunderstood and thought Tripp was settling down. The look of bald hope in eyes that were so much like Tripp's made Adrianna reconsider.

She'd heard the rumors that Frank Randall's health was failing. There were few secrets in Jackson Hole, especially in the medical community. Everyone knew Tripp's dad had been diagnosed with melanoma and hadn't had a good response to the initial treatment.

Adrianna had been shocked and saddened to hear the news. Not only because Frank had been a driving force for civic improvements and conservation in Jackson Hole for many years but because he was also Tripp's father. She knew what it was like to lose your dad.

"You were saying," Kathy prompted, a smile trembling on her lips.

"Tripp hasn't proposed." That much at least was true. Adrianna saw no need to tell Kathy that she was certain the thought had never entered her son's mind.

A look of relief crossed his mother's face. She reached over and patted Adrianna's hand. "I feel confident it won't be long."

Once again Adrianna let a tiny smile and a slight lift of one shoulder serve as her response.

The waiter brought out their food and the talk turned casual. Then, when a small boy at a nearby table created a ruckus, the lunch conversation shifted to children.

"Have you thought how many children you'd like?"

Adrianna breathed a sigh of relief. Although personal, it was a general topic she could handle. After all, Kathy wasn't asking how many children she'd like to have with *Tripp*. "I always thought I'd like three."

"Frank and I had three." A wave of sadness crossed Kathy's face. "Our oldest, Frank Jr., died of SIDS at ten months. Then Tripp and Hailey came along."

"I didn't know you'd had another child," Adrianna said sympathetically. "I can't imagine what losing him must have been like."

"We were devastated," Kathy admitted. "Even after all these years the pain is still there. Just like I'm sure it hurts when you think about your parents."

Adrianna thought back to the phone call, the rush trip back to Wyoming from college, having to make the funeral arrangements, the two caskets at the front of the church...

It wasn't long until the tears welling in Adrianna's eyes matched the ones in the woman's eyes sitting across from her. She cleared her throat and blinked rapidly.

"Like you said, when someone you love dies—especially unexpectedly—it's difficult." Adrianna pushed her plate aside, no longer hungry.

"Well, don't we make a fine pair?" Kathy gave a choked laugh. "We go out for lunch and end up crying. I'm sorry I brought up your parents."

"Don't be," Adrianna said with surprising vehemence. "No one mentions them anymore. It feels as if they never existed. But they did exist. I like talking about them."

"That's how I sometimes feel about Junior. He was such a sweet baby." A wistful look crossed Kathy's face. "There are times I'm reminded of something he did and I'd like to mention it, but I don't want to make anyone uncomfortable."

"Tell me." Adrianna leaned forward. "I'd love to hear about him."

Emotion had Kathy's eyes going soft. "Only if you also tell me about your parents. I don't think I had the pleasure of meeting them."

The lunch that Adrianna had planned to last less than an hour ended up going closer to two. By the time Kathy looked at her watch and yelped that she had to get back home to Frank because Hailey had plans, Adrianna realized not only had they both eaten their quiches, but they'd also had dessert.

The slight headache she'd started the day with had completely vanished.

"I really enjoyed getting to know you better," Adrianna said as they walked to their cars.

"I feel the same." Kathy looped her arm through Adrianna's and gave it a squeeze. "Our lunch has solidified my belief."

Adrianna lifted a brow.

"You are the perfect woman for my son."

When Adrianna walked into Tripp's office Monday morning and shut the door, Tripp wasn't sure what to think. His thoughts couldn't help but rewind to Saturday night when she'd kissed him.

Perhaps she'd come to apologize. Or to tell him the kiss had been great after all. He grinned at the thought.

"Is this a good time?" she asked.

"Depends on what you have in mind."

She must have taken that for assent because she crossed the room. He watched her cast a curious look at the bookshelves he'd had put in this week. He thought she might comment on them. Instead she met his gaze. "You and I need to talk."

Tripp inwardly groaned. He knew he should have told Jim Ferris that he and Adrianna were only friends. He also should have called her Sunday and thanked her for going with him to the party. That would have been common courtesy.

He hadn't told Jim because there hadn't been a good opportunity and he hadn't called Adrianna because he didn't want to make whatever there was between them seem like more than it was...simply two friends attending a work-related function together. Of course, kissing wasn't usually a part of those types of evenings, but there were exceptions to every situation.

"May I have a seat?"

He pulled his thoughts back to the brunette who stood before him in heels and a yellow dress topped by a white lab coat. Good God, she was beautiful.

"Certainly." He gestured to one of the two wingback chairs that faced his desk.

She dropped gracefully into the nearest chair and crossed her long, slender legs. "There's something I need to discuss with you."

"Look, I admit I should have called and thanked you for going to the barbecue with me." Tripp ignored her startled expression and plunged ahead. He'd learned long ago the best defense was a good offense. "But I didn't want to give the wrong impression."

The second the words left his mouth, and her lips tightened, he wished he'd kept his mouth shut. Or perhaps he should have started with why he hadn't informed Jim as he'd promised.

"You didn't want to give the wrong impression." She spoke slowly and distinctly, crossing her arms in the process. "What *wrong* impression would that be?"

"Uh, that I was interested in you?" Instead of getting out of the hole he'd dug, he felt himself sinking deeper.

"Oh." Adrianna lifted a perfectly arched brow. "Because I'm desperate or because you're such a hot guy?"

"No. No." Tripp couldn't believe this conversation had gotten so out of control. "Not true."

"Which part?"

"What do you mean?"

"Which part isn't true?"

"You're not desperate."

"What about the other part?"

He grinned. "Well, I am kind of hot."

To his relief, Adrianna smiled.

"I think I'm a great kisser."

Her smile vanished.

The ground beneath his feet that had started to solidify began to rumble and buzz.

Adrianna pulled a phone from her lab coat and glanced at it for a second before dropping it back into her pocket. "I don't have long, so I'll get to the point."

Tripp shifted in his chair, disturbed by the seriousness of her expression.

"Your mother and I had lunch yesterday." Adrianna paused. "She believes you're on the verge of popping the question and she wanted me to know that I have her and your father's blessing. In fact, they'd like it if we got married as soon as possible. It appears seeing you settled is something that would make your dad very happy."

He took a moment to let the words sink in. Tripp couldn't imagine his mother doing something like this. "What did you say?"

"I told her you hadn't popped the question."

Tripp raked a hand through his hair. "What kind of response is that?"

"She took me by surprise. I didn't know what else to say," Adrianna said indignantly. "I like your mother. I didn't want her to feel foolish. You're her son. You should be the one to tell her that I'm only a friend."

It was the only solution, but Tripp already knew she wouldn't take the news well. Gayle had been gone only a year when he'd started to receive pressure to jump back into the dating pool. Now, three years after her death, the subtle pressure had turned blatant.

Adrianna was right. Honesty was the only option. And the clarification needed to come from him.

"I'll speak with them tonight." His lips twisted. "I apologize for my mom putting you in such an awkward position."

"Your mother is a wonderful woman," Adrianna stressed. "I really enjoyed visiting with her. I feel badly that we deceived her, even if it was inadvertent."

Tripp was surprised by her passionate defense of his mother. While Gayle and his mom had gotten along, in this case he had no doubt she'd have blamed his mother for putting her in the middle.

Adrianna rose with a graceful elegance. "I need to get to L & D."

Tripp walked her to his office door. "Thanks for going to the party with me."

Her lips twitched. "I'd tell you I had fun, too, but you might take it wrong and conclude I'm after your hot bod."

"How could I?" He hid a grin. "Not after what you told me about my kissing."

"I like your books," Adrianna said, not rising to the bait. "You might want to reread the one by Jim Collins. It's a classic."

Her phone buzzed again. After glancing at the readout, Adrianna took off down the hall without a backward glance.

When Tripp stepped back into his office, he headed straight to the bookshelf to look for the book she'd recommended. It didn't take him long to find it.

He lifted it from the shelf, read the title and laughed.

Good to Great.

CHAPTER SEVEN

It was the day that would never end.

After leaving Tripp's office, Adrianna spent the rest of the afternoon in labor and delivery. Two of her patients had presented in labor at the same time.

By the time the second baby finally made his appearance, it was close to nine o'clock and not only had Adrianna skipped lunch, but she'd missed dinner as well. She pulled into her driveway with a stomach growling so loudly it drowned out the country song on the radio.

She didn't notice the truck at the curb until she was at the door of her ground-floor condo and found Tripp sitting on the small iron bench.

"Where have you been?" he said in lieu of a greeting.

"Oh, honey, did I forget to call?" she said in a mocking tone, fatigue wrapping itself around her shoulders like a heavy blanket.

"I've been waiting here for...hours."

She gave him a long, measured glance.

"Okay, maybe closer to twenty minutes." He stood, looking more like a rancher than a CEO in his chambray shirt, jeans and boots. "But I *was* worried."

"Two deliveries." Adrianna pushed open the door and flipped on the lights.

Tripp followed her into her condo. "Everything go okay?"

"Two healthy baby boys." Adrianna dropped into the closest chair and kicked off her shoes. "Something tells me you didn't come all the way over here to ask about my day."

"I went to speak with my parents tonight."

Adrianna straightened in the chair. All evening she'd wondered how his conversation with his parents had gone. She hoped he'd been gentle and that he'd stressed to his mother that she'd genuinely enjoyed their conversation. "And?"

"My dad was having a bad day." Worry turned Tripp's blue eyes a cloudy gray. "My mom had been up most of the night and was exhausted. I stayed with him while she took a nap."

"I'm sorry to hear that." Adrianna resisted the urge to reach over and touch his hand. "He looked so good at the barbecue."

"I wish I knew what's going on." Tripp closed his eyes for a second. He took a deep breath, then let it out slowly. "He's seeing the doctor tomorrow."

"It's okay if you didn't get a chance to do any talking."

"Oh, we talked plenty," Tripp said with a humorless laugh. "Mostly about you. They're very impressed."

"With me?"

"Of course with you."

"What did they say?" Adrianna asked.

"How wonderful you are, so nice and sweet." Tripp looked at her with an odd look in his eyes. "What did you and my mother talk about?"

"You mean other than you?"

He nodded. "She must have told me a thousand times what a compassionate person you are."

Adrianna thought back to their conversation. She'd felt such a connection with Tripp's mother. "We talked about my parents dying. Stuff like that."

She could tell Tripp sensed there was more, but he didn't push.

"My dad told me how happy he was that I'd found someone. He said he'd been worried about me." Tripp turned away from her searching gaze, but not before she saw the sheen of tears in his eyes. "He said, he told me, that he could now die happy."

He jerked to his feet and moved to the window, staring out into the darkness.

"Oh, Tripp." Adrianna rose and went to him. "I'm so—"

He whirled, his jaw set in a stubborn tilt, his blue eyes flashing. "I told him he's not going to die. That he's going to get better. That one day he's going to dance at my wedding."

She saw the fear in his eyes and realized that Tripp loved his parents every bit as much as they loved him.

"That could very likely happen," she said in the soothing tone she usually reserved for women in labor. "I've heard good things about the new chemo regimen they have him on."

"I couldn't tell them we aren't together." His gaze met hers. "I tried, but I just couldn't do it."

"I understand." She offered him a reassuring smile. "It sounds like tonight just wasn't a good night for that type of conversation."

"No, I mean I can't do it. It will break their hearts."

Adrianna could only stare as his words registered. "You have to tell them, Tripp. They'll find out sooner or later we're not together."

"Why do they have to find out?"

"I'm not following you."

"We could date." He spoke fast, the words tumbling out one after the other. "Just for a little while," he added, apparently seeing the look in her eyes.

"Tripp, I adore your parents—I really do." Adrianna took a deep breath and chose her words carefully. "But I won't participate in a charade. I can't lie to them."

"I didn't say lie to them." His jaw took on a hard edge. "I said we could date. Are you saying you don't want to date me?"

"We've been down this road before." Knowing how upset he was, Adrianna gentled her tone. "I don't interest you and—"

"I never said that," he countered before she could continue.

"Yes, you did. That's okay, because..." Even though she didn't like to lie, she had to protect herself. How could she face him every day at the hospital if he knew she was carrying this torch for him? The answer was, simply, she couldn't. "Well, because you don't interest me."

She'd lied to him before on this issue, but never had she said it quite so plainly.

He searched her eyes. "Tell me you don't have any feelings for me. Not even as a friend."

"Well, as a friend—"

"You're my friend, too," he said.

"Tripp, I'm not going to lie to your parents and make believe we have a relationship that doesn't exist."

"I'll pay you," he said, the desperation blanketing his face matching the tone.

"I'll pretend I didn't hear that."

"Adrianna, I'm not asking you to do this for me." His almost-frantic gaze met hers. "Do it for my mother. For my dad. Give them a little happiness."

"It isn't right."

"What isn't right is having the ability to give those two people some measure of comfort and not doing it."

"Spell it out. Tell me exactly what you're proposing." The second the words left her lips, she knew she'd lost the battle.

"We start dating. I tell my parents we're not talking marriage at this time but I enjoy your company. Which I do," he hurriedly added. "In a month or so, when my dad is better, I tell them we had a falling-out and are no longer together."

"Why not tell them that now?"

"Because my dad will be better, stronger in a month." *

You hope. I hope.

"We're talking thirty days," Adrianna repeated, wanting to make sure they were clear on this point.

"One month," he said, his gaze never leaving hers.

Adrianna considered his proposition for a long moment. Even if she met someone today whom she was drawn to, the odds were he'd still be available in thirty days. She found the thought of spending the next month in Tripp's company alternately appealing and scary as heck.

Would she be able to keep her feelings hidden? Would she be able to keep herself from falling in love when her feelings for him already ran so deep? It was a lot to consider.

Still, in the end, it was really so little to ask. If she was in his situation, she'd appreciate someone helping her out.

"What about Jim Ferris?" she asked. "You already told him we weren't together."

Tripp shifted uncomfortably from one foot to the other. "I didn't get a chance to speak privately with him the other night."

"Tri-ipp."

"Hey, but it's worked out for the best." He turned a beseeching gaze on her. "You'll do it, won't you, Adrianna? For my parents. For me."

"Yes," she said with a sigh. "For your parents."

His blinding smile caused her heart to skip a couple of beats. "Remember, this is just between us. No one can know this is a charade. That includes any of our friends."

"I can't do that." Adrianna shook her head. "I can't lie to Betsy."

Tripp's smile disappeared. "It's only for a month."

Adrianna lifted her chin. "She's my best friend."

She heard Tripp take a deep breath, then let it out slowly. He searched her eyes and she saw the question reflected in the blue depths.

"She won't tell anyone," Adrianna assured him, "if that's your concern."

"It is a worry." Tripp raked a hand through his already-disheveled hair. "Jackson Hole isn't that big. My parents can't find out—"

"—that we mean nothing to each other." Adrianna finished the sentence for him, a knifelike pain lancing her heart.

His gaze went sharply to her. "I hope you don't believe that. I consider you a good friend."

The warmth mixed with the worry in his eyes made her feel better. Perhaps this one-month charade would end up being a blessing in disguise.

Perhaps at the end of four weeks, Tripp would find it impossible to let her go. Perhaps he'd realize that he'd found what he'd been looking for, right under his nose. Perhaps—

Yeah, and perhaps pigs could really fly.

Adrianna resisted the urge to snort at the girlish dream. In one month she would walk away. Then she'd begin her search for Mr. Right in earnest.

Adrianna was grateful that her monthly book club met on Tuesday night. Because she and Tripp had just come up with their plan yesterday, she wouldn't have to deal with any questions.

As she walked up the steps of Cole and Margaret Lassiter's mountain home, her fingers tightened around the plate of hummus-stuffed celery sticks topped with capers.

Although all these women were friends, she'd only recently started attending the book club. Betsy—who'd never met a stranger—had told her the discussions were super fun and had begged her to join.

Finally, several months ago, Adrianna had agreed to give it a try. Although she found the meetings enjoyable, she still felt a bit like an outsider. Because of Betsy just having her baby, tonight would be the first time she'd attended without her close friend by her side.

It will be okay, she told herself as she balanced the plate in one hand and rang the bell. At least she was prepared for a book discussion.

Of course, that was assuming no one wanted to discuss *The Garden of Forking Paths* and instead opted for a general discussion on what everyone was currently reading.

She was debating whether to ring the bell again when the door swung open.

"I'm sorry to keep you waiting." Margaret smiled with a warmth that melted away Adrianna's unease. "Charlie was entertaining everyone with a magic trick he's recently mastered."

Charlie was Margaret and Cole's eight-year-old son. They'd adopted him several years earlier when their mutual friends had been killed in a horrific car crash just outside of Jackson. Margaret had opened a physical therapy clinic in town last year and with Cole busy running his Hill of Beans coffee empire, many wondered if they'd delay having more children.

Margaret's rapidly growing midsection answered that question.

"How are you feeling?" Adrianna asked the woman everyone referred to as Meg.

"Fabulous." Meg slipped her arm through Adrianna's. "Cole and Charlie spoil me terribly. I'm loving every minute of it."

"Well, you look wonderful," Adrianna said sincerely.

Over the years the red hair that Meg had eschewed as a young girl had deepened to a rich auburn, the vibrant color a perfect foil for her creamy complexion. She was tall and slender, the hunter-green stretch-fabric maternity dress showing her only extra weight was in her belly.

"So do you."

The admiration in Meg's eyes when she looked at Adrianna's color-blocked shirtdress in taupe and orange was too real to be faked.

Before Adrianna could respond, Meg squeezed her arm. "I'm glad you decided to dress up a bit."

"With five children, I'm lucky to be dressed," Mary Karen Fisher called out as Adrianna and Meg entered the great room where they were meeting. "Forget stylish."

With blond hair pulled back in a ponytail and dressed in jeans and a floral top, Meg's sister-in-law looked more like a college girl than a mother of five little ones. With a sunny personality and an infectious laugh, everyone liked Mary Karen, including Adrianna.

"I'm all about stylish." Lexi Delacourt straightened from where she'd been bent over the refrigerator. Her tailored navy suit did little to enhance her curves. "But I got off late and had to come straight from work."

"Does that mean no pasta rustica tonight?" Adrianna tried to hide her disappointment.

In addition to being a well-respected social worker, Lexi was a gourmet cook who usually made the entrée for the book-club dinner meetings. She'd mentioned last time that she planned to make pasta rustica with chicken sausage and three cheeses this month. The dish was one of Adrianna's favorites.

Lexi smiled. "I had a feeling my day might be a long one, so I dropped the casserole off on my way to work. Meg just put it in the oven to warm."

"Wine?" Meg asked, holding up a glass and a bottle.

Adrianna demurred. "I'm on call tonight, so iced tea or water is fine."

Meg smiled. "Coming right up."

"I know Betsy isn't coming." Mary Karen took a sip of wine. "And July has a sick kiddo. Who else is skipping?"

"Kate and Joel are out of town," Lexi said.

"Michelle won't be here," Adrianna informed the others. "She went home early because she wasn't feeling well."

"We can still have a good discussion with four of us." Meg glanced around the table. "Would you mind if Charlie ate with us? Cole should be home shortly."

After everyone reassured her that they'd be upset if the boy *didn't* join them, Meg set an extra place at the table and called in the child, who still wore a magician's cape and hat.

When his mother replaced the capers with raisins and deemed Adrianna's dish "ants on a log," Charlie ate the appetizer with great enthusiasm.

Over dinner, the four women talked about everything from movies to their favorite phone apps. When the talk shifted to the benefits of cloth diapers over disposables, Adrianna felt out of step.

She hoped that someday diapers would be a part of her world. There was plenty of time yet. She wasn't even thirty. She had several patients in their early forties pregnant with their first baby.

Adrianna took sympathy on Charlie, who seemed equally bored by the conversation about pocket diapers versus all-in-ones or all-in-twos. "Tell me about your magic tricks."

Charlie was intently explaining to her how he'd made the bead vanish from the paper cup and show up in his pocket when he heard the front door open.

"Daddy's home." The brown-haired boy jumped to his feet and raced from the room.

"We have extra food in here," Meg called out. "If you're hungry."

The sound of heavy footsteps sounded on the hardwood. From the rumble of deep voices, Adrianna guessed that Cole Lassiter wasn't alone.

She half expected to see him with Ryan. After all, he and Betsy's husband were best friends from way back. Until she remembered Ryan would be home tonight with his wife and newborn son.

The second Tripp stepped into the room, Adrianna's heart stopped beating.

No, the voice inside her head cried out, it's too soon for the charade to begin.

At first, it appeared she may have been granted a reprieve. Meg busied herself preparing a plate for the two men, while Lexi got them each a beer from the refrigerator. Charlie was talking nonstop to his dad about his magic tricks. And Tripp was teasing Mary Karen about something related to her boys. Then his gaze shifted.

When her eyes met his, she realized he hadn't expected to run into her this evening either. The smile lifting his lips told her he was far better at reacting to unexpected changes than she was.

"Anna." He crossed the room and bent down. Before she could react, he kissed her cheek. "I didn't know you'd be here. But then, I was tied up in meetings all day."

The eyes of the three women in the room appeared to widen at precisely the same instant.

"Anna?" Mary Karen sputtered. "Only Betsy calls her Anna."

Lexi's gaze shifted from Adrianna to Tripp. "Is something going on between you two?"

Tripp laughed, his hand resting on Adrianna's shoulder. "What was your first clue?"

Meg smiled. "I always thought you'd be a perfect match."

Cole chuckled. "My wife, the matchmaker."

"I just want everyone to be as happy as we are," Meg said with sudden seriousness.

Adrianna gazed up at Tripp. When he looked at her that way, she couldn't help but blush. Her cheek still sizzled from the warmth of his lips. What would it be like if he really kissed her? Not the chaste kisses of the other night, but ones fueled by passion?

Then she reminded herself that none of this was real. He was only pretending to be happy to see her. Deep down, he was probably irritated he'd been forced to put their game plan into play so soon.

The gentle kiss on the cheek wasn't real. The way his hand lingered on her shoulder as he played with her hair wasn't real. The only thing that *was* real was her response to his nearness.

Her heart had picked up speed. Heat washed across her cheeks as desire uncurled and stretched in her belly. That was when Adrianna realized the hardest thing about this charade wasn't going to be making people believe she cared about Tripp. It was going to be walking away from him when the month was over and finding a way to mend her broken heart.

CHAPTER EIGHT

Once the men left to go upstairs to Cole's office, Adrianna tried to forestall the inquisition by beginning a discussion of *The Garden of Forking Paths,* sure that Lexi would take part. No such luck. Then she brought up the romance novel she'd recently read. Not one bit of interest. Not when they had a love story right in front of them.

"When did this thing with you and Tripp happen?" Lexi pinned Adrianna with her gaze. "It had to have been recently."

The other two women were equally focused.

Adrianna rose to her feet and started clearing the table. "Well, you know we went to that hospital function at the country club together. Then he invited me to a barbecue at Jim Ferris's house last Saturday."

Lexi took several plates from her hands and gave them to Meg, who was loading the dishwasher. "Yes, but I thought that was just as friends."

"Friendship has a way of turning into something more," Mary Karen pointed out, obviously thinking back to her own romance with her husband, Travis. Her lips curved up in a smile. "It's such fun when that happens."

"Cole and I had to find our way back to an earlier friendship." Meg's eyes took on a distant glow. "Yeah, it was fun, but stressful, too. Not knowing if we were just together because of Charlie or because our feelings went deeper."

"Is that what's happening with you and Tripp?" Lexi asked.

"I've liked Tripp since I was in high school," Adrianna admitted. "Back then he only had eyes for Gayle."

Lexi cocked her head. "That was his first wife, right?"

Even though Lexi had been a Jackson Hole resident for a number of years, she hadn't grown up in Wyoming.

Adrianna nodded. "Gayle and I were next-door neighbors."

"She was beautiful. But no more beautiful than you," Mary Karen added hastily.

"Gayle was a lovely person inside and out." Adrianna's exhalation came out sounding more like a sigh.

"She's been gone three years," Mary Karen said gently. "It appears he's finally ready to move on."

"That's what he says." Adrianna forced a light tone.

"You don't believe him?" Lexi's gaze turned sharp and assessing even as her eyes filled with concern.

"I want to believe," Adrianna heard herself whisper.

She wished she could tell them that she'd always known Tripp was *the* guy for her. Even back in college when she'd convinced herself she was in love, those emotions had been child's play compared to what she felt for Tripp.

Meg moved to her side and gave her arm a squeeze. "Give it time. This is new for both of you."

"Believe me, there were so many times that I said to myself that no way would Travis Fisher and I ever be together." Mary Karen's eyes then took on an impish gleam. "I'm the best thing that ever happened to him. Just ask me."

The women laughed and the talk turned to men and how they often didn't know what was best for them until it bonked them over the head.

Adrianna felt the tension slip from her body and she realized she felt close to these women. They were her friends. They cared about her.

Mary Karen filled their cups with coffee and Meg brought out the dessert: a banana-split cake that was Charlie's favorite.

Adrianna had never even heard of such a thing. It was a layered dessert, not really a cake and without any ice cream. The butter cookie crust was followed by an "ice-cream" filling of butter, vanilla, eggs and confectioner's sugar. Meg had added toppings of bananas, pineapple, strawberries, shaved chocolate and nuts. Maraschino cherries added some bright color.

Over bites of the delicious confection, Mary Karen informed them that instead of an end-of-summer barbecue, she and Travis had decided to host a retro party. There would be Twister, spin the bottle and plenty of mistletoe, a staple of any party at the Fisher household.

"Make sure you put it on your calendar, Adrianna," Mary Karen urged. "With all that mistletoe, you'll want to be there with Tripp."

"Mistletoe. Party?" Tripp said from the doorway. "I'm there."

"I was telling Adrianna about the retro party at our house. Everyone else already heard about it over breakfast Sunday. But you two weren't there." Mary Karen tried to look severe but failed.

Every Sunday, their particular group of friends got together after church, while the children were in Sunday school, at a local café, The Coffeepot.

Adrianna knew that Ryan and Betsy used to meet everyone for breakfast before their son was born, but she'd never been sure she was welcome. Until now. A warmth flowed through her veins.

"When's the party?" Tripp asked.

Mary Karen gave him the date and he glanced at Adrianna.

It was well within the one-month timetable of her and Tripp's romance and it would definitely be odd if they didn't attend.

"I think it sounds like great fun," she said. "I'll be there."

"We'll be there." Tripp smiled at her, his tone slightly chiding. "You're part of a couple now, sweetheart."

Couple. Sweetheart. The words were bittersweet.

If this was real, she'd be on top of the world. But it wasn't. Being with Tripp in a fake relationship was like having a maraschino cherry in reach but only being able to look, not touch.

"Well—" Adrianna pulled to her feet "—this part of the couple needs to head home. I have a busy day tomorrow."

"I'm so glad you came." Lexi gave her a hug, then whispered in her ear, "I have a good feeling about you and Tripp."

"Come back anytime." Meg's eyes were warm "Don't be such a stranger."

The words only confirmed her earlier realization. She had been keeping everyone at arm's length. She'd always been more reserved, but she'd taken a step back after her parents had died. Once the scandal erupted...

"I'm leaving, too," Mary Karen announced, moving to the door. She shifted her gaze to Tripp. "If you and Adrianna decide to have a big family, Travis and I will be happy to give you a few pointers."

"Good to know," Tripp said with an easy smile.

"I had a perfectly lovely time," Adrianna told her hostess.

"I did, too." Mary Karen giggled. "Especially because we didn't have to discuss *The Garden of Forking Paths.*"

"Adrianna, call me," Lexi called out from her seat in the great room. "We'll do lunch."

"I will." When Adrianna turned toward the door, Tripp turned with her.

He looped an arm around her shoulders. "I'll walk you to your car."

"Not necessary." The words left her mouth before she realized they hardly sounded like a woman falling in love.

"It is unless you want me to kiss you right now in front of everyone," Tripp said with a wicked grin.

Adrianna felt her face warm. "Come on, then."

Tripp chuckled. "As you can see, she's quite infatuated with me."

She jabbed him with her elbow. An audible *oof* escaped his lips. He quickly rallied and caught up with her, taking her hand and waving a quick goodbye to Cole, Charlie and her friends.

Once the door closed behind them, he released her hand.

"I think that went well." He sounded quite pleased with himself.

"I was shocked to see you."

"I could tell."

"Meg said Cole was at work and then all of a sudden you show up with him."

"If you're asking if I came over deliberately knowing that you would be here, the answer is no," Tripp said in a casual tone. "He mentioned something about his wife having some women over for a book club, but it didn't register."

"Why were you with him?" The second the words left her mouth she realized she'd overstepped. After all, where Tripp went—and for what reason—wasn't any of her business.

Tripp just smiled. "Cole wanted to show me what the P.I. has uncovered. Ryan will use the information in his efforts to get Keenan's case reopened."

"I didn't know Cole was so heavily involved."

"Cole is bankrolling much of the costs," Tripp said. "Even with Ryan donating his time, there are still court fees and a detective doesn't come cheap."

Adrianna remembered her friend's despair when Keenan was convicted. "Betsy would be over the moon if he was freed."

"So would I." Tripp's blue eyes turned serious. "Keenan is a friend and a good guy."

"What I don't understand is why he wouldn't let anyone help him earlier. Why did it take two years behind bars?"

Tripp shrugged, but she had the feeling he knew exactly why.

They reached her Subaru and he opened the door for her. Instead of slipping behind the wheel, Adrianna turned, resting her hand on the top of the door. "Even though we want to make everyone believe our relationship is real, there's no need for you to go overboard."

"Surely you're not referring to that simple kiss on the cheek?" His lips twitched. "Adrianna, that's the kind of kiss I'd give my grandmother."

"Oh." Adrianna didn't know what else to say. It had felt like more at the time, but perhaps she was the one who'd overreacted.

"Going overboard would be doing something like this."

Before she knew what was happening, he'd wrapped his arms around her and pulled her to him. Curling a finger under her chin, he lifted her face and closed his lips over hers.

The kiss started off slowly and she decided this wasn't so bad. A nice little kiss like they'd shared before. Unlike that night, this time Tripp didn't step back.

Like a volcano that had lain dormant for many years and was beginning to stir, the longer the kiss continued, the hotter it burned. Something clenched low and deep in her belly. When his tongue swept her lips, she opened her mouth to him.

Suddenly close wasn't close enough. She laced her fingers through his hair and pressed her body against his. They fit perfectly together.

Where she was soft, he was hard. Very hard.

She abruptly pulled back, her heart pounding, her lips tingling and her body aching with need.

"Good night." She gave him a little shove back and slid behind the wheel of her car, pulling the door shut.

She paused for a couple of seconds before starting the vehicle. When she realized she was waiting for him to say anything—or do something—she cursed herself and turned the key.

She lifted her hand in a wave and drove off, leaving Tripp standing beside the driveway, a strange look on his face.

Perhaps he was wondering what had just happened. She understood his confusion. She hadn't expected such passion between them.

Oh, she'd once hoped for such a thing, but had given up on that long ago. Of course, she'd learned the hard way that lust didn't equal love.

It was a lesson she'd be wise to keep in mind.

The next day, Tripp found himself daydreaming through two important meetings. The heat that had exploded between him and Adrianna last night had been a surprise.

Okay, maybe not that much of a surprise. She was a beautiful, sexy woman. Ever since he'd moved back to Jackson Hole, there had been something in the air between them. Something he tried very hard not to think about.

While he'd been married, despite Gayle's unfounded accusations, he'd never given Adrianna—or any other woman—a second thought. Yet, now he couldn't stop thinking about the very woman Gayle had accused him of secretly wanting.

Tripp raked a hand through his hair. Perhaps this thirty-day thing wasn't such a good idea after all. If only his mother hadn't been so happy when she'd stopped by his office yesterday.

He knew his parents wanted him to find someone special, to get married again and give them some grandbabies. They couldn't understand that lately his job had kept him too busy for serious dating. They'd find it even more difficult to understand that once he had time, that woman could never be Adrianna.

Tripp knew it made no sense, but in his mind, to be with her would somehow lend credence to Gayle's accusations.

He told himself there were hundreds of other single women in Jackson Hole.

But they're not Adrianna.

Tripp shoved aside the thought and refocused on the problem at hand. Kissing Adrianna had reawakened the desire he'd thought had died with his wife. Which meant he had to proceed carefully. The last thing he wanted was to hurt her. Even though she never spoke of her past relationships, something told him she'd experienced difficult times. Perhaps she was still carrying a torch for some long-ago boyfriend.

A knife twisted in his chest. Not because he was jealous but because he didn't like the thought of someone hurting her. Despite her cool, composed demeanor, Adrianna was a sensitive soul. That was why his protective instinct had reared up when Winn Ferris started showing an interest in her.

A knock sounded at his door and he glanced up.

Speak of the devil.

"Winn." Tripp rose to his feet, forcing a friendliness he didn't feel into his voice. "Come in."

Why the heck hadn't Paula told him Winn was in the outer office? He could have come up with some excuse about a meeting.

"No one was at the desk, so I thought I'd see if you had a few minutes." Winn strode into Tripp's office as if he owned the place. Dressed in a dark suit with a gray shirt and tie, he looked every inch a successful businessman.

"You caught me between meetings." Tripp gestured to a pair of large leather chairs. "Have a seat."

Instead of retreating behind his desk, when Winn sat, Tripp settled himself into the matching chair. "What brings you to the hospital this morning?"

"I need some help," Winn said, looking surprisingly serious.

"Dad suggested I speak with you."

Tripp knew the mention of Jim Ferris, chairman of the board of trustees, had been deliberate. Whatever Winn wanted, alluding to the fact that his father had specifically thought he could help his son almost guaranteed he'd get what he wanted.

Unless, of course, he wanted Adrianna.

"I'll be happy to help." Tripp kept his tone even and a smile on his lips. "If I can. But if it's about golf-course development, that's outside my purview."

"Let me give it to you straight." Winn leaned forward, resting his forearms on his thighs. "My father has a good rapport with the older, more established members of the community. I need access to the younger, influential ones. That way I can learn first-hand their concerns about the development I'm proposing. I'll know what information to provide to assuage those concerns."

"Where do I fit in?" Tripp had a sinking feeling he knew where this was heading, but just in case he was wrong, he didn't want to assume.

"Dad tells me that you've got a lot of friends in this town."

"I grew up here," Tripp acknowledged.

"Your friends are considered to be part of the new breed of movers and shakers. Men like Nick Delacourt, Gabe Davis, Cole Lassiter, Ryan Harcourt and Joel Dennes. Not to mention all the physicians."

Tripp found it interesting that Winn had only mentioned the men in the community, not any of the influential women.

"What exactly are you getting at?"

"I'm not part of that group," the dark-haired man said bluntly.

"Most of the men you've mentioned belong to the Jackson Hole Young Professionals Organization. They're also active on various chamber of commerce committees."

"I'm aware of that." Winn waved a dismissive hand. "I don't have time for committees and clubs right now."

"To get something out of organizations, you do have to put in time" was all Tripp said.

"Again, let me give it to you straight."

"By all means."

"I want you to get me invitations to all the social events this group of yours holds." Winn's eyes never left Tripp's face. "That way I'll get to know these people and be able to pick their brains."

Tripp started to shift in his seat, but stopped himself just in time. This was worse than he'd imagined. "Winn, I'm sure you understand that unless it's an event I'm personally hosting, I have no control over the invitation list."

"I don't believe you." Winn's lips lifted in a sardonic smile. He rose to his feet and strode to the window overlooking the Elk Refuge. After several seconds he turned. "One word from you would get me an invitation. We both know that. Dad wasn't in favor of your being chosen for this position. That's something else we both know. But he's been supportive and set aside his personal feelings."

"Go on," Tripp said when Winn paused.

"If you refuse to help me, if you try to sabotage my entry into this group, I'm afraid my father will see you as someone who's holding a grudge against him. I think he might be disappointed enough to make sure the other members of the board are aware of this as well."

"You're threatening me." Tripp was no stranger to such politics. While he wasn't surprised that Winn would do something like this, it disturbed him that Jim would stoop to this level.

"*Threat* is such an ugly word." A slight smile lifted the corners of Winn's lips. "And totally inaccurate. I'm simply making you aware of what might possibly happen should you choose to decline my request. I came here to ask a favor of a man I consider a friend."

Tripp rose to his feet once more and reviewed his options. He wasn't at all cowed by the man's threats, but he'd learned long ago to think before rashly responding.

"Rumor has it Dr. Fisher and his wife will be hosting a retro party in the next week or two. Getting an invitation to that event would be a good first step."

Tripp made a great show of glancing at his wrist. "I'm going to have to cut this short. I have a meeting at noon."

"I appreciate your time," Winn said with a smooth smile. "Just remember, if word gets back to my father that you've told your friends about our little arrangement, well, he won't be pleased."

A knock on the door sounded.

"Come in."

"Mr. Randall, the meeting you have scheduled—" His personal assistant, Paula, paused, her eyes widening. "I'm sorry. I didn't realize—"

"That's okay, Paula." Tripp walked to his office door. "Mr. Ferris is leaving."

"I'll be seeing you soon, Randall." Winn strolled across the room, that irritatingly smug smile still on his lips. "Be sure and give Adrianna my best."

Paula waited until Winn was out the door to speak. "I didn't mean to run him off. Actually, your noon meeting has been canceled."

"That's okay," Tripp assured her. "We'd completed our discussion."

"If you're sure..."

"I am."

"I'm sorry I wasn't at my desk when he arrived."

"No worries."

"Shall I put him on the list?"

Tripp knew she was referring to the list he'd given her of people whose calls he always wanted to take.

"Uh, no," Tripp informed her. "Mr. Ferris is more of a business acquaintance than a friend."

After his visit today, that category was where he was going to stay.

CHAPTER NINE

The building that housed the ob-gyn offices where Adrianna practiced was within a short walk of the hospital. If she forgot to bring her lunch, Adrianna usually walked over and had a salad in the cafeteria.

Today, she decided to entirely bypass the hospital. The truth was, she didn't want to take the chance of running into Tripp. The scorching kiss of the other night had muddled her thinking. She didn't want to see him until she had time to process what had happened.

Instead, she headed downtown to Hill of Beans for her favorite nonfat iced latte and a side salad. When she saw the crowd she almost turned back, but decided it would take her longer to walk somewhere else. Besides, any place at noon was bound to be busy.

Thankfully, the line moved quickly. While most of the customers were getting their lunches and coffees to go, Adrianna planned to stay. But by the time she'd gotten her food and paid, the tables were full.

She was ready to ask for a to-go container when a woman seated by the window waved her over.

"You can sit with me if you'd like," the dark-haired young woman dressed in a maternity business suit offered.

"Thank you. I'd love to join you." Adrianna recognized the woman as Karla Anderson, one of her patients.

Karla had recently moved back to Jackson Hole from Kansas City to take a job in county government. At the moment, that was about all that Adrianna could remember about her. Other than, of course, she was six months pregnant.

Adrianna placed her salad and latte on the table, then stowed her tray before taking a seat.

"You just missed your boyfriend," Karla told her.

Adrianna froze. "Who?"

"Tripp Randall." Karla raised a glass of tea to her lips. "Someone at work was telling me today that you two are a couple."

Adrianna should have been surprised that news would travel so fast, but she wasn't. "Was he alone?"

Karla nodded. "He got his food to go. I'm surprised you weren't meeting him for lunch."

"I wasn't sure how long the delivery I had this morning would take," Adrianna said smoothly. "How have you been feeling?"

"I have more energy," Karla said. "Although, I'm still having some trouble sleeping...but I think that's stress."

Adrianna lowered her voice. "Are you still working long hours?"

Karla had taken a position as a community planner and had been practically living at the office for the past two months.

"Work is actually going better." Karla took a sip of tea. "It's my personal life that's in the toilet."

Adrianna knew very little of Karla's home situation, other than she was single and the baby's father didn't live in the area. She'd gently tried to probe for more details—believing that the more she knew, the better she could treat the whole person—but

Karla had put up a brick wall. Today, it appeared that wall stood on the verge of crumbling.

"I'm sorry to hear that," Adrianna murmured.

"Justin—he's the baby's father—has been pressuring me to return to Kansas City," Karla said with a sigh.

Adrianna dipped her fork into the salad dressing she'd gotten on the side, then stabbed a piece of romaine before responding. "Is that where he lives?"

Karla nodded. "He wants us to be a family. Or so he says."

Adrianna chewed thoughtfully for several seconds, then took a sip of latte. "You don't believe him?"

"He's still hung up on his old girlfriend." A look of sadness swept over Karla's pretty face. "They'd dated for years. They were even engaged once."

The scenario reminded Adrianna of Tripp and Gayle. Except Tripp had married his childhood sweetheart. "What happened?"

"She got cold feet. Told him she wasn't sure he was 'The One.' Suggested they date around." Karla heaved a heavy sigh, her large brown eyes dark with pain. "I got him on the rebound. The day I found out I was pregnant, he told me she'd come to him, wanting to get back together."

Adrianna's mouth dropped open and her heart went out to the young woman sitting across the table. "How horrible."

Karla gave a humorless laugh. "I wished him well, told him I was pregnant and that I'd be moving back home to Jackson Hole."

"What did he say?"

"He said he wanted to be with me." Tears filled Karla's eyes but she blinked them back. "I knew he was only saying that because I was pregnant. He adored Chelsea. In my mind I used to call her Saint Chelsea because I'd never heard him say anything but positive things about her."

"Is there a chance he meant it when he said he wanted to be with you?"

Karla shook her head. "I found out from a friend that when she told him she wanted him back, they slept together."

Adrianna reached across the table and squeezed Karla's hand. "I'm so sorry this happened."

"It could be worse." Karla lifted her chin. "At least I have family and supportive friends here. In fact, your boyfriend's sister, Hailey, is a good friend from high school."

"What a small world" was all Adrianna could manage to say. Hearing Tripp referred to as her boyfriend still blew her away.

"You're so lucky." Karla's voice was laced with envy. "I wish Justin cared for me half as much as Tripp seems to care for you."

Adrianna smiled and took a bite of salad. For the next month, pretending was the name of the game.

If only she could stop herself from wishing it was real.

"You didn't need to ask me to come with you tonight," Adrianna whispered to Tripp as they approached the entrance to the Wildlife Museum on the edge of Jackson.

The rustic building was lit up like a Hollywood premiere. Dark-suited men sauntered through the door with women attired in swishy cocktail dresses.

Adrianna hadn't expected to see Tripp until the weekend. But he'd called her when she'd gotten home from the hospital on Wednesday night and asked her to attend the Thursday event. Because she was supposed to be his girlfriend, how could she refuse?

Besides, she'd heard a lot about the special exhibit that had been brought in and she wanted to be one of the first to see it. And heck, she might as well be honest and admit that she wanted to see Tripp, too.

She'd finally put the kiss into perspective. It had been a

momentary lapse on both their parts, fueled by a game that for that moment had seemed a bit too real.

"You look lovely tonight." Tripp's gaze lingered on the dark green chiffon cocktail dress and silvery strappy sandals that added another three inches to her height.

She'd considered putting her hair up for the event, but in the end had settled for pulling the sides back with some shimmery clips. "You're looking pretty spiffy yourself."

The second the words left her mouth, she wished she could pull them back.

"Spiffy?" Tripp's lips quirked upward.

Heat rose up Adrianna's neck. "My father loved the word *spiffy.*"

"Well, I feel honored that you would use it to describe me," Tripp said, sounding surprisingly sincere.

There was no more chance for conversation as they walked through the entrance. It appeared the entire population of Jackson Hole had decided to come out for the opening of the exhibit.

There were stations scattered throughout the museum serving champagne and wine. Waiters holding silver trays passed through the crowd offering a variety of appetizers including spinach-and-brie artichoke hearts and chicken-and-pepper egg rolls.

Although Tripp snagged an egg roll, Adrianna shook her head.

"Not hungry?" Tripp raised a brow.

"Not really." Adrianna grasped Tripp's arm when a man making his way through the crowd pushed up against her.

"That's better." Tripp winked and Adrianna felt heat rush through her.

"Now we look like a real couple," he added and her warm feeling disappeared as quickly as it had arisen.

Still, it was a good reminder. This wasn't really a date. This was her—and him—playing a part.

"Are your parents...?"

The question hadn't even had a chance to leave her mouth when she saw Frank and Kathy across the room. Although Tripp's father looked a little tired, overall, he appeared better than the last time she'd seen him. His mother, dressed in a black linen cocktail dress, practically glowed with happiness.

Kathy saw her at the same instant. Her smile broadened and she waved, then tugged her husband's sleeve and pointed.

Almost immediately the two began making their way across the room.

"Your parents are on their way over," she said to Tripp.

A pleased smile lifted his lips. "Dad must be feeling better if they're here."

Adrianna released her hold on Tripp's arm when his parents drew close. "Mr. Randall," she said. "Mrs. Randall, how nice to see you."

A look of dismay crossed his mother's face. "What have we told you about Mr. and Mrs.?"

Adrianna smiled shyly. "Kathy and Frank, how nice to see you."

"That's better." Kathy surprised Adrianna by giving her a quick hug. "I'm sure my son has already told you, but I'll tell you again—there's not a more beautiful woman in this museum tonight than you."

"Ah, no, actually, he hasn't said that," Adrianna said in a teasing tone, gazing up at Tripp through lowered lashes.

"I told her she looked lovely," Tripp said in mock outrage. "I didn't want to be too effusive. She might decide she deserves someone better than me."

"There's no one better than you," his mother said, her expression turning serious. "But we women like compliments. Isn't that right, Adrianna?"

"Sincere compliments are always appreciated." Adrianna kept her tone light. She'd been such an ugly duckling most of her growing-up years that it was still hard for her to accept she now had a few swanlike characteristics.

"It does my heart good to see you two out together." Frank may have spoken to both of them but his gaze was fixed on Adrianna.

"Tripp and I have fun," Adrianna said, not knowing how else to respond.

"You're exactly what my boy needs."

If Adrianna was being honest she'd tell his father that she wasn't sure that was true. Tripp was an outgoing guy, a man comfortable in any social setting. She took her time warming to people and was more shy than gregarious.

"I heard you're going to help Winn get acquainted with the younger crowd," his dad said to Tripp.

Adrianna resisted the urge to frown. She'd gotten the distinct feeling that Tripp didn't care for Winn. Why would he help him get acclimated to the community?

"We talked about it yesterday," Tripp said, his expression giving nothing away.

"I know you don't care much for Jim," Frank said. "But I'm happy you and Winn have hit it off. Jim cares a lot about his boy and your friendship with him will go a long way toward helping you build a good relationship with his dad."

"Are you and Winn buddies now?" Adrianna asked, unable to conceal her surprise.

"I believe I may have misjudged Winn initially," Tripp said smoothly.

"I think we all know why," Frank said with a laugh.

Kathy and Adrianna both glanced curiously at him.

"Winn was coming after your woman." Frank gave Adrianna a wink. "That would cause any man to rustle up his spurs."

"He was simply being nice," Adrianna murmured, embarrassed by the discussion.

"Honey, that man had his eye on you." Frank smiled with satisfaction. "But you picked the better man, no doubt about it."

"Speaking of better men—" Tripp reached over and took Adrianna's hand "—this man better be doing a little socializing before the silent auction begins."

After saying their goodbyes, he and Adrianna began making their way through the crowd, stopping every few feet to speak with someone they knew.

Even though Tripp appeared oblivious to the attention they were attracting, Adrianna caught lots of surreptitious glances directed their way. Who would finally capture the wealthy bachelor's heart had been the subject of much speculation from the moment Tripp had returned to Jackson Hole.

She wondered if he knew all the talk this charade of theirs was generating. Even if he did, she doubted he cared. All that mattered to him was his parents' happiness. That love of family was one of the many reasons she loved him.

The second the word crossed her mind, she banished it to the hinterlands. She liked Tripp. Liked him a lot. When she was younger, she was convinced she loved him.

Now she realized what she'd felt had been a version of puppy love. He was so cute and so nice, what teenage girl wouldn't have fallen in love with him? Adrianna now realized there needed to be more to a man than a sexy smile.

To truly love someone, you had to know them. While she and Tripp were casual friends, she didn't really know what made him tick. Like his suggesting they participate in this charade. Until that moment she hadn't realized quite how important his family was to him.

No, she didn't *love* Tripp Randall. She didn't know him well enough to love him. For some reason the realization made her feel better.

They'd just finished speaking with the mayor and his wife

when Adrianna heard Tripp mutter an expletive under his breath.

"What's the matter?" she asked in a tone low enough for his ears only.

"Winn Ferris." His own voice was more of a growl.

Adrianna looked up to see Winn striding across the room with the two of them firmly in his crosshairs. She smiled, then turned to Tripp. "You told your parents you were buddies."

Okay, perhaps he hadn't used the word *buddy,* but what he'd said gave that impression.

"I lied." Tripp's jaw set in a hard angle even as a smile lifted his lips.

"Why?"

"I'll tell you when we're alone." Tripp held out his hand when Winn drew near. "Fancy running into you here."

"This is the place to be tonight," Winn said smoothly, shaking Tripp's hand before shifting his gaze to Adrianna. "Aren't you a vision of loveliness in that dress. You put all the other women in the room to shame."

"Hello, Winn." Adrianna couldn't help but smile. The man was full of it, but she liked his style.

"Can I get you something to drink?" Winn asked solicitously as if she was his date, not Tripp's.

Tripp's scowl told Adrianna that fact hadn't escaped his notice.

"I'm fine," she said. "It was nice seeing you, Winn."

Adrianna closed her fingers around Tripp's arm and spoke to him as though they were alone. "There's someone I want you to meet." She turned to Winn. "I'm sure we'll see you later."

She didn't even give Winn a chance to respond, but pulled a quite willing Tripp through the crowd.

"Who do you want me to meet?" he asked, appearing mildly curious.

"No one," she said.

"No one? You told Winn—"

"Did you want to spend more time with him?" she asked as they turned the corner and entered a room displaying Native American folk art.

"Not at all."

"That's what I thought." Adrianna paused to look at a piece of intricately painted pottery. "Like a good girlfriend, I extricated us from the situation."

"Well done, Ms. Lee."

His approving smile sent warmth sluicing through her body.

"I may just have to keep you around," he added in a teasing tone.

"I'm yours for a month," she murmured.

Tripp stepped close and brushed a strand of hair that had come loose back from her face. "I have a feeling that time is going to go by way too quickly."

Her breath stopped, then began again, ragged and unsteady. "What a sweet thing to say."

His eyes darkened and his hand lowered to her shoulder.

Her body tightened in anticipation. Was he really going to kiss her here, surrounded by all these people?

"There you are."

Kathy Randall's words were like a splash of cold water. Adrianna took a step back as heat flooded her cheeks.

"Ohmigoodness." His mother's gaze shifted from Adrianna to her son. "Did I interrupt something?"

"Not at all," Tripp said smoothly. "Adrianna and I were just having a private discussion."

Frank covered his snort of laughter with a cough.

"When I saw you I meant to invite you both for dinner tomorrow. But it completely slipped my mind." She shifted her gaze to her son. "I'm making pot roast."

From the way she looked at Tripp, Adrianna guessed it must be one of his favorites.

"Tomorrow is Friday night, Mother."

"I know you two will probably be doing something," Kathy said, not appearing deterred by his lack of enthusiasm. "I thought we could eat early, say around six, which will still give you the entire evening to do, well, whatever it is you have planned."

Adrianna wondered why Tripp was hesitating. If he wanted to spend more time with his dad, having dinner seemed a perfect way to do it. "I love pot roast."

"Perfect." Kathy's smile was blinding. "We'll see you at six."

"What did Winn want—" Frank began.

"Honey," Kathy said, "we've monopolized them enough this evening." Her eyes began to twinkle. "Let's let them get back to their, uh, discussion."

"Sorry 'bout that." Frank gave his son a wink, a smile tugging at the corners of his lips. "Carry on."

Adrianna wanted to melt right through the floor.

"I feel like a sixteen-year-old kid caught making out on our living room sofa," Tripp said, shaking his head. "Except this time, instead of discouraging the intimacy, they're encouraging it."

"Did they ever catch you and Gayle making out?" Adrianna wasn't quite sure why she asked. Unless it was to remind herself that what he and Gayle had shared was special, while what she and Tripp shared was simply a business arrangement.

Tripp gave a halfhearted laugh. "A couple of times."

Adrianna simply smiled, not sure how to respond.

"How about you?" Tripp asked after a long moment. "Did your parents ever walk in on you and a guy?"

"Actually..." Adrianna paused, embarrassed by the admission she was about to make, yet not sure why. Lots of girls didn't date in high school. "I never brought a guy home. I wasn't much into dating when I was younger."

The sad fact was, boys hadn't been into her. It was humiliating enough to not have had a date until college without adding that little detail. Even more humiliating to recall once she had started dating how she'd let herself be played, even though she'd been old enough to know better.

"Now that you say it, I don't remember seeing you at any of the high school dances."

It was kind of him to act as though he'd noticed her back then, when they both knew she was about as far off his radar as one could get.

"So no make-out sessions on the couch? Ever?"

Adrianna sighed. "Not a one."

"We'll have to remedy that situation."

Adrianna froze. Was he suggesting that they, that the two of them...make out? She resisted the urge to fan her flaming face.

"Start walking." Tripp took her arm. At her startled look, he smiled. "Mrs. Wieskamp from the hospital auxiliary is headed in our direction. Once she gets started talking about her cats, it's hard to get away."

Adrianna liked wrapping her hand around Tripp's hand. Even though she'd attended several of these types of events either alone or with Betsy or other friends, it felt good to be part of a couple.

Oh, who are you kidding? You like being with Tripp.

By the time the event began winding down, Adrianna had to admit that it was Tripp who'd made the evening memorable. He wowed her with his knowledge of folk art, and with him laughing at some of her pithy one-liners, she felt positively brilliant.

People whom she'd felt uncomfortable with—probably because they were shy like her—blossomed under Tripp's genuine interest and friendliness. By the time they walked to his truck, she felt as if she'd made some new friends.

"That was fun," she said, when he reached around and opened the passenger door for her.

"You sound surprised."

"I guess I am," she admitted. "Normally these events are a chore for me."

"Why is that?"

"I'm shy," she told him, although she felt certain it was something he'd already observed. "It's hard for me to make small talk."

Even as he slipped behind the wheel, he shook his head. "You have to be making that up. You appear so at ease."

Ah, no, that was him.

"Thank you for that compliment," she said, flushing with pleasure. "But you make it easy. You're so good with people. You seem to genuinely care."

"I like people," he admitted, backing up the truck and heading down the steep drive back to the highway. "And I do care. I guess that's one of the reasons I'm toying with the idea of running for office."

Adrianna pulled her brows together and cocked her head. "What office?"

"Mayor of Jackson," he said in a matter-of-fact tone.

She couldn't hide her surprise. "Really? You're interested in politics?"

"I have been for a long time," he admitted, sounding almost embarrassed by the admission.

"I'm surprised Gayle never mentioned that to me."

Tripp's smile disappeared. "Her stance on the issue was too little money for too much work."

"Oh." Adrianna wasn't sure what to say, though she had to admit that comment sounded like Gayle. "Well, I'm impressed. The town would be lucky to have you."

Tripp appeared touched. "Thank you for that."

"You'll make the right decision."

"I'd like to be able to have an impact on all the changes the town will be facing," he said, almost eagerly. "The problem is, I enjoy what I'm doing. I'm not sure I'm ready to give that up."

A chill traveled up Adrianna's spine as something occurred to her. "When you're a politician, every aspect of you and your family's life is under scrutiny."

"You're right about that," he said with a laugh. "Good thing I don't have anything to hide."

"Yeah," Adrianna said faintly, "good thing."

It was a good thing that she wasn't really his girlfriend and that there was no chance she'd ever be his wife. While he might not have anything to hide, she did.

CHAPTER TEN

Although Tripp had assured Adrianna that dinner in the Randall household was a casual affair, she couldn't bring herself to show up in jeans. Because the area was still in the throes of Indian summer, she chose a flirty tan dress with rust-colored flowers and a pair of Espadrille wedges.

Tripp showed up on her doorstep in a pair of worn denim jeans and a graphic T-shirt. She liked him this way. When she saw him at the hospital his hair was always carefully controlled, but tonight the blond strands were allowed to be wild.

On the way over to his parents' ranch, she had to fight the urge to run her fingers through those silken curls.

"Are you sure you don't mind going over to Ryan and Betsy's house later tonight?" she asked Tripp when they pulled into the long lane leading to his parents' home.

Betsy had called earlier and asked if Adrianna wanted to come over in the evening. She could tell her friend was shocked when she said that she had plans with Tripp. Apparently, none of the women at the book club had spilled the news.

When Betsy had told her to bring Tripp along, Adrianna had called him at work to see if he was interested.

"Going over there is perfect," Tripp said. "It's just the kind of thing a couple dating would do. It'll give me a chance to catch up with Ryan on the latest with Keenan and you and Betsy can have your time."

She wanted to tell him that a date wasn't where one person went off with their friend while the other person did the same, but then she reminded herself they weren't on a date. Not really.

"Thanks for agreeing to come to dinner," Tripp said when they reached the front door. "I know it means a lot to my parents."

"I like them," Adrianna said. "And I like pot roast."

By the time they finished with dinner, Adrianna realized what she'd told Tripp when they'd arrived had been an understatement. She *loved* his mother's pot roast.

"That was a fabulous meal," Adrianna told Kathy as they relaxed at the table over apple crisp and coffee. "I can't remember when I've had better."

"I can't tell you how happy I was when I learned you weren't a vegetarian."

Hailey shot her mother a warning glance.

"I mean, it would have been fine if you were," Kathy hastily added. "But in this family we love our beef and pork."

At first Adrianna didn't make the connection until she remembered that Gayle had been a vegetarian.

"Well, it was wonderful," Adrianna said.

The momentary silence that settled over the table was broken by Hailey.

"Karla told me she's so excited that you're going to deliver her baby," Hailey said.

Kathy raised a brow. "Which Karla are we talking about?"

"Karla Anderson," Hailey explained. "You remember her. She and I ran in the same groups in high school."

Because of confidentiality concerns, anytime someone

mentioned one of Adrianna's patients, she was careful in what she divulged.

"I ran into Karla at Hill of Beans," Adrianna told Tripp's sister. "We had lunch together."

"Karla Anderson is pregnant?" Surprise crossed Kathy Randall's face. Her gaze settled on her daughter. "I didn't realize she was even married."

"Oh, Mom." Hailey smiled. "You don't have to be married to be pregnant."

"You do in this family," her dad said from the other end of the table, shooting his daughter a pointed gaze.

"Well, Karla thought she'd found a great guy but he wasn't. She tossed him back into the dating pool." Tripp's sister added a big dollop of homemade whipped cream to the top of her dessert.

"Tossed him back?" Tripp frowned. "Like the father of her baby didn't even matter?"

"I'm probably not doing a good job of explaining it." Hailey turned to Adrianna. "If I get it wrong, just correct me."

Adrianna gave a noncommittal smile and took a sip of coffee. She had no intention of discussing Karla's personal life over the dinner table. If Hailey wanted to spill all her friend's secrets, that was up to her.

"Justin—he's the baby's father—had been engaged to this girl named Chelsea before he met Karla. She's this goddess and Karla always worried he was still hung up on her."

Hailey paused to take a bite of apple crisp.

"What happened?" Her mother rested her arms on the table, her own dessert forgotten.

"The day Karla discovered she was pregnant, Justin told her Chelsea wanted him back."

"Did he want Chelsea?" Kathy asked.

"I guess so." Hailey shrugged. "Anyway, Karla moved back to Jackson and Justin is in Kansas City. He keeps calling and pleading with her to move back, but she doesn't want to be second best."

A silence settled over the table.

"That would be hard," Kathy said finally. "I'm glad you're not in that situation."

"Pregnant?" Hailey said. "Or with a guy who's hung up on another woman?"

"Both," Kathy said at the same time as Frank, and they all laughed.

Adrianna joined in the laughter, although she didn't find anything particularly funny about the situation. Karla's story hit a little too close to home. She noticed Tripp's smile appeared strained.

Was he thinking what it would be like if his baby sister was in that situation? Or was he remembering Gayle and realizing that anyone who came after her would always be second best?

"I was so surprised when you told me that you were going out with Tripp this evening." Betsy stroked the soft red fur of her Pomeranian, Puffy, who sat cuddled on the sofa beside her.

The baby had been fed and burped and put to bed shortly after they arrived, and the last time they checked, had been sleeping soundly.

Even though Ryan and Tripp were in the other room, Betsy kept her tone low, as if concerned about being overheard.

Adrianna leaned forward. "I'm going to tell you something, Bets, but you have to promise me to keep this confidential. You can't tell anyone. Not Lexi or July or Kate—none of our friends."

Betsy's brows drew together. "Can I tell Ryan? We don't keep secrets from each other. He won't tell anyone."

Adrianna thought for a second. "Okay, but swear him to secrecy, too."

"What's going on, Adrianna?" Betsy's voice shook. "I have to admit you're scaring me."

Adrianna gave a little chuckle. "There's nothing scary about it, Bets. It's just kind of sensitive."

"Well, don't keep me waiting. Spill."

"Tripp and I aren't really dating." Adrianna found herself embarrassed by the admission. "His parents got this idea we were a couple. You know his dad has some serious health issues. Well, we didn't want to tell him it wasn't the case and make him feel badly—"

Betsy's entire face pulled together in a frown. "You're going to do the fake-dating thing indefinitely? Until he gets better or until he—"

"No, of course not," Adrianna said quickly. "It's just for a month. Hopefully his dad will be doing better by then. But no matter how it's going, at that point, we'll break up and go our separate ways."

"You know I've always thought of you as one of my smartest friends." Betty spoke slowly and deliberately. "But I'm having trouble making sense of this arrangement."

"Perhaps I didn't explain it well enough." Adrianna took a deep breath and tried again. "Tripp's parents got the mistaken impression that we were a couple. His mother even invited me for lunch one day and told me how happy she was that Tripp had found someone, how happy that had made his father, who was going through some difficult times."

Betsy opened her mouth as if to speak, but Adrianna continued, wanting to make sure she laid all the facts on the table for her friend.

"Tripp was going to tell his parents that they were mistaken, that he and I were simply good friends. When he went to their home, his dad was having a bad day and he couldn't do it."

"What about your plans to find someone special?" Betsy sneaked in the question when Adrianna paused to take a breath.

"That's why we decided on the thirty days," Adrianna said. "If I did meet someone during these four weeks, the odds are they'd still be around when Tripp and I broke up."

She flashed a triumphant smile, satisfied she'd explained the situation in such great detail that Betsy couldn't help but understand and agree with her.

The worried lines remained on Betsy's forehead. "I think this could work."

Adrianna exhaled the breath she'd been holding. "I knew you'd unders—"

"*If* you thought of Tripp as only a friend."

Adrianna glanced nervously at the doorway. "I do think of Tripp as a friend."

"I didn't say 'as a friend.'" Betsy spoke slowly and distinctly. "I said as *only* a friend."

Was that pity she saw in her friend's eyes?

"I know how much you like him, Adrianna," Betsy whispered. "I worry you're going to become even more attached to him during these four weeks. When it ends, you'll be heartbroken."

"I'm not a child, Bets," Adrianna snapped, her words uncharacteristically tight and harsh. "I know the score."

"I knew the score with Ryan." Betsy lowered her voice even more. "It was still hard to be around him when he thought he was in love with you."

Adrianna shifted uncomfortably in her chair. "He never really loved me."

"I know that now." Betsy's tone told Adrianna she was confident in her husband's love. "But working for him, going out with him so he could be close to you was pure torture. Isn't it hard for you to be around Tripp and not touch?"

Adrianna thought of the kiss they'd shared and tiny flames flickered to life in her belly, sending heat coursing through her veins. Her face warmed.

Betsy's eyes widened. "Have you and he—"

"No. No," Adrianna said more forcefully. "We've kissed, that's all."

A look that Adrianna couldn't quite decipher flickered in the back of her friend's eyes. "Tripp kissed you? Or you kissed him?"

"Well, actually..." Adrianna hesitated.

"It's a simple question."

"Okay, I kissed him once. And he kissed me once. Oh, twice."

A tiny smile tugged at the corners of Betsy's lips. "Was that for show?"

"What do you mean?"

"Were there people watching? Is that why you did it?"

"No. I can't remember why we did it, actually."

"Just a spur-of-the-moment kind of thing?"

"Exactly." Adrianna liked that explanation. "It didn't mean anything."

"Of course, it didn't," Betsy said in a matter-of-fact tone. "I've changed my mind. I think this one-month thing with Tripp is a good idea."

Adrianna breathed a sigh of relief. "You understand why it is we're doing this?"

"Of course."

"For his parents' sake."

Betsy smiled. "No need to say more. Just know I understand and you have my full support."

After Ryan finished updating Tripp on what was going on with Keenan's appeal, they headed down the hall to Nate's room. Even though his friend had checked on his new son only minutes earlier, Ryan wanted to make sure Nate was sleeping comfortably before they joined Adrianna and Betsy in the living room.

The Winnie the Pooh night-light cast a golden glow over the

nursery. It was identical to the small light Gayle had purchased for their baby's room only days before she died.

Tripp forced himself to breathe in and out. Even though thinking of the loss of Gayle and their baby girl no longer brought tears to his eyes, he'd accepted that the pain would always be with him, lurking in the background, ready to surprise him at moments like this.

He shifted his gaze to his friend.

Ryan was staring at the baby with a look of wonder on his face. This man, who had numerous awards for his bull-riding skill, was gazing at his son as if he was the most precious gift he'd ever received.

Would he ever have that experience? Tripp wondered. Would he ever find a woman to take Gayle's place—

No. He stopped the thought before it could fully form. If he did find someone down the road, she wouldn't be a replacement for Gayle. That wouldn't be fair.

From the time they'd been in middle school, it had been him and Gayle. Initially, being with her had been so effortless. It had gotten more complicated when her parents split during her senior year.

Her father had been cheating on her mother for years while on business trips. When the truth came out, there was an ugly divorce. That was when Gayle had begun to change. Every time Tripp even so much as looked at another girl, she'd accuse him of wanting to take her to bed. No matter how much reassurance he tried to give her that she was the only one he wanted, it wasn't enough.

In college, he'd gotten fed up and suggested they see other people. When Gayle had dissolved in tears and promised to change, he'd realized he loved her too much to walk away. Still, while their relationship had been good, it had never been great.

Tripp had finally come to the conclusion that his expectations must have been too high. Not every couple could be as close as his parents.

"He's fast asleep," Ryan said in a low tone. "Shall we join the girls?"

"The girls" were laughing and chattering about some new movie trailer they'd recently seen. Tripp had seen the trailer. It looked like the standard chick flick with a small amount of action thrown in. Not his kind of movie at all.

"You'll have to tell me how you like it," Betsy told her friend, smiling up at Tripp when he took a seat beside Adrianna on the love seat.

When Ryan sat next to his wife, Puffy bared her teeth. But his friend simply smiled fondly at the dog and firmly placed the small puffball on the other side of him, putting his arm around his wife.

It occurred to Tripp that if he and Adrianna were truly dating he'd be putting his arm around her, too. Just to be convincing, he followed Ryan's lead.

He inhaled the pleasing sultry scent of her perfume and made a mental note to let her know again how much he liked the fragrance once they were alone.

"I'll probably go see it tomorrow night," Adrianna said.

For a second Tripp was confused until he realized she was still talking about the movie. "Tomorrow is Saturday."

"I often go to movies on Saturday night," Adrianna informed him, looking confused.

"I know what you're doing tomorrow night," Ryan said with a broad grin. "You're seeing a chick flick."

The former-championship-bull-rider-turned-attorney gave a loud oomph as Betsy's elbows connected with his ribs. "If we didn't have a newborn, we'd be joining them."

Adrianna's eyes widened and Tripp saw the second she realized that if they were really dating, they'd be at the theater...together.

"Who do you usually go with to the movies?" Tripp asked, feeling a twinge of what felt like jealousy but couldn't be. Because, after all, he and Adrianna were only friends.

"Betsy and I used to see a lot of them together. Michelle and I used to go together, too, before she got married." Adrianna lifted her chin. "Lots of people go to the movies alone."

While Tripp guessed that was probably true, she was his girlfriend for the next month and the idea of her having to go to the movies alone didn't sit well with him.

"It looks like it has some action scenes in it," he said. "I bet I'll like it."

Adrianna cocked her head. "What are you saying?"

"I'm saying let's go to the movies tomorrow night...together."

CHAPTER ELEVEN

While the movie theater in downtown Jackson wasn't bursting at the seams, Adrianna and Tripp did have to wait in line to get tickets. When they got to the window, Adrianna pulled some bills out of her purse. Tripp waved them aside.

She thought about pressing the issue, but decided they could settle up later. Once inside the fifties-era lobby she started to head for the seats when Tripp reached out and grasped her arm.

"First we need popcorn," he said with an enticing smile.

With visions of calorie-laden kernels dancing before her, Adrianna began to shake her head. Then she realized being with Tripp at the movies had been something she'd dreamed about during those high school years when he was dating Gayle and she was sitting at home...alone.

She'd envisioned their sitting in the back row with their bags of popcorn, laughing and talking. Even though she'd been painfully shy, in her dream she'd been extremely witty. By the time the movie started, he'd put his arm around the back of her seat and she'd lean close....

"Earth to Adrianna."

She jerked her thoughts back to the present and found Tripp gazing at her, a tiny smile pulling at his lips. "Popcorn?"

Adrianna nodded. "I'd love to share yours."

"What about a soda?"

Ugh. She rarely drank the stuff, but tonight, hearing the word from his lips, it sounded so tempting. "Just a sip of yours will be enough for me."

Even though he didn't look shocked, she realized seconds too late what she'd done. She'd made the assumption that he would want to share his drink with her. How unsanitary.

"We can see if they will give us an extra cup," she said hurriedly, following him to the concession line. "I didn't mean to imply that you would want to drink after me."

He shifted his entire body toward her and that devastating smile was once again directed at her. His gaze dropped to her lips. "I don't mind drinking after you. After all, it's not as if we haven't already—"

"What can I get you, sir?" The high school–aged girl behind the counter asked.

"Your popcorn-and-soda special, please." Tripp pulled some bills from his pocket.

This time Adrianna didn't protest but merely added it to the tally she was keeping in her head.

"Where do you want to sit?" he asked when they entered the darkened theater. "Toward the front? Or back?"

"I like the back row," she said with uncharacteristic boldness. Hey, even if this wasn't a replay of that long-ago dream, at least she'd be sharing popcorn with Tripp Randall in the back of a theater. Now if she could only manage to utter a few witty comments...

"Sounds good to me." He stepped aside to let her enter the empty row.

She moved all the way to the center, settling into the soft red cushioned seat while breathing in the clean, fresh scent of Tripp and his yummy cologne.

Not yummy, she told herself immediately—musky. *Yummy* implied she wanted to eat him up, while really the only thing she wanted to eat was the popcorn.

Yeah, right.

The trailers for upcoming movies hadn't yet started, so there was plenty of time for witty conversation and pithy one-liners. The trouble was, with her bare arm brushing Tripp's she was finding it difficult to think.

Perhaps she shouldn't have worn a dress tonight, especially the sleeveless one she'd chosen. She'd picked it because she liked the spice color and she had a tan open-knit cardigan that could easily be added if the night turned cool.

Now, sitting beside Tripp, she was very aware of how much skin was exposed. Each time he glanced her way, little rushes of heat flashed over her exposed flesh.

Tripp extended the bag of popcorn to her.

She shook her head. "In a minute."

He lifted a kernel and held it out. "At least try a bite. Then we'll both have popcorn breath."

She had to laugh. Instead of reaching out and plucking the kernel from his fingertips, Adrianna opened her mouth.

His eyes widened a fraction before turning dark. He leaned close.

When her lips closed over the kernel, they caught a bit of his fingers and heat shot straight to her belly.

She savored the kernel, reveling in the rich taste of the butter and the bite of the salt...and remembered how his fingers had tasted in her mouth.

By the time the theater darkened and the trailers began, she couldn't have said what they'd discussed. She'd made him laugh— she knew that. He'd made her laugh, too. It was the kind of laugh that alluded to the tension building in the air between them. A kind of anticipatory heightened awareness that caused her pulse points to thrum and her body to stand ready on high alert.

Perhaps it was only her imagination but a couple of times when Tripp looked at her, she felt as if he was finally seeing *her.* Not as Gayle's friend, not as a medical professional, but as a woman. From the heat in his eyes, he liked what he saw.

They were watching the last trailer when the words that had been poised on Adrianna's lips since they'd first taken their seats slipped out.

"I used to have this fantasy about being kissed in a movie theater," she heard herself confide.

For a second, Tripp's sharp intake of breath was his only response. Then he handed her the cup of soda. "Have a sip."

Even though she wasn't at all thirsty, Adrianna took the cup. She told herself to be relieved he'd chosen to ignore her inappropriate comment. As she took a bigger-than-planned sip of the cola, she acknowledged it wasn't relief coursing through her veins but disappointment.

His eyes remained firmly focused on her as she drank, then handed the cup back to him. Never wavering in his gaze, he took a sip, then set the popcorn and soda aside.

"When I watched your lips against that straw, all I could think about was how much I wanted to feel them pressed against my mouth."

Adrianna blinked. Had she just hallucinated? Or had Tripp Randall actually said he wanted to kiss her?

"What's stopping you?" she said softly.

The words had barely left her lips when he pulled her close and his mouth closed over hers. She wrapped her arms around his neck and drank him in. Unprepared for the intensity of the heat engulfing her, only the sound of the movie's theme music starting and a distant titter of laughter kept Adrianna from crawling over the seat divider and into his lap.

When the kiss ended, she was breathing hard as if she'd just run a long race. She was grateful for the darkness, relieved they were in the back row and that no one had noticed their inappropriate behavior.

Tripp gave a halfhearted laugh. "For a second I felt as if I was sixteen again."

His eyes glittered in the darkness and testosterone wafted off him in waves. He may have recognized the necessity of stopping but it made her feel good to know he hadn't wanted to pull back any more than she did.

"Thank you," she said.

A puzzled look crossed his face. "For what?"

"I'd always wanted to kiss a boy in the back of the movie theater." She forced a light tone, making it sound as if it didn't matter which boy—er, man—she kissed. The truth was, it mattered. "Now I have."

Even though the movie had begun, he didn't look at the screen and neither did she. There was a sense of waiting in the air.

"Always happy to further your education," he said in a low tone.

Adrianna felt her cheeks warm even as she waved a dismissive hand. "It isn't as if there are *that* many things I missed out on. Though, I never did make out with a boy in a car either."

Eek. Why not just issue him a formal invitation? One that said, "Your presence is requested in the backseat on a deserted dirt road"?

A spark flashed in his eyes. "Really?"

Too late, she turned her attention back to the screen and pretended to be interested in the movie. "Not important."

He leaned close, his voice low enough for her ears only. "I think it is. You missed out on a vital part of a teenage girl's education."

"Forget I said anything." She resisted the urge to turn her head, knowing his mouth would be right there.

"I'll try." He rested his arm on the back of her seat. "But I can't promise anything."

~

For being a romantic comedy, the movie was fairly good. But Tripp found it difficult to concentrate. He blamed it on the fact that they were sitting in the back row. Every red-blooded American male knew there was only one reason to sit in the back of a theater, and it wasn't to watch the show.

Being in the last row surrounded by empty seats was a unique experience. Even though the ones down front and partway back were filled, there were at least seven empty rows in front of them.

It wasn't simply the fact that he was sitting alone in a dark room with a pretty woman at his side. He'd gone to plenty of management conferences and had sat next to many attractive females. He'd never felt the urge to kiss any of them senseless.

There was something about Adrianna that pulled him in. Sure, she was one of the most beautiful women he'd ever known. But it was more than that. She was just as beautiful on the inside. There was also an innocence, a sweetness about her that brought out his protective instincts.

Protective instincts? His lips curved upward in a slight smile as he tried to make himself focus on the movie. *Protective* wasn't the word for how he felt as he inhaled the sultry scent of her lotion.

The skin of her shoulder was warm and soft beneath his fingertips. He couldn't help but wonder if the rest of her would be equally soft. The instant his mind leaped to the image of her naked beneath him, he forced it away.

Okay, maybe he lingered on the image for a second or two but that was all. A full-blown sexual relationship between him and Adrianna would only complicate their friendship. Even though

Tripp knew there was no future in such intimacy, he couldn't help wishing things could be different.

A little kissing in a car, well, that wasn't quite the same thing as getting naked. Lots of friends kissed. Although, at the moment, Tripp couldn't think of any women friends that *he'd* kissed. He felt certain—or at least fairly certain—that it happened a lot.

Adrianna chuckled.

He quickly slanted a glance in her direction but her eyes were on the screen. At least one of them could say they'd actually watched the show.

All Tripp could think about was how she'd *specifically* mentioned the fact that she'd never parked with a guy. He felt honored that she'd trusted him with that unfulfilled desire.

After all, if she'd have told Winn about this particular desire, there was no doubt in Tripp's mind that Winn would have been all over her. Tripp clenched his teeth together.

Winn had no subtlety, no finesse. If that man took Adrianna parking, he'd ruin her fantasy.

Tripp, on the other hand, would know just how to make it a memorable experience for her.

His lips lifted in a smile. Yep, he'd make it good for her. Something told him it would be a night neither of them would soon forget.

"Where would you like me to take you?" Tripp said, after they'd exited the theater and stepped out onto the sidewalk.

Adrianna jerked her attention to him. "Take me?"

His smile was boyish and went straight to her heart. "Would you like some dessert? Or a drink? Or..."

His voice trailed off and her heart skipped a beat.

It would really be simplest to choose a glass of wine or perhaps a bite of tiramisu. But Adrianna had always had a curious streak and she couldn't help but wonder what was behind door number three.

Don't ask, the voice of reason in her head whispered. *Do. Not. Ask.*

Several people smiled at Tripp and stopped to talk. She wondered what they thought about seeing the CEO of their hospital dressed in faded blue jeans and a twill shirt. Personally she thought he looked—because she'd permanently barred the word *yummy* from her vocabulary, she substituted—*very handsome.*

The casual conversation they'd engaged in should have made it easier to pick door one or door two. Instead, a curious humming filled her body and she felt almost as if she was a race-car driver positioned in the starting gate with engine revving.

"Finally," Tripp said in a low tone when the last person had walked away. "What would you like to do?"

"I'd like to know what's behind door number three."

A confused frown wrinkled his brow and she bit back a groan.

"I mean the third alternative," she hastily explained. "You gave me the choice between dessert, a drink, but then we were interrupted when you were going to give me the third alternative."

While that wasn't quite accurate, it was close enough to the truth.

He took her arm and pulled her to the side of the building. "I'm not sure if what I'm about to suggest is appropriate."

"Who cares?" Adrianna said in a flippant tone. "Say it anyway."

He trailed a finger up her bare arm. "We could use the rest of this evening to further your education."

Adrianna licked her lips. "What exactly did you have in mind?"

"Well—" he took a step closer, although there was hardly any room between them now "—you were already kissed in the back row of a movie theater, so you've had that experience. But you've never gone parking. We could get that crossed off your to-do list tonight if you're interested."

Interested? No, of course she wasn't interested.

"Sure," she heard herself say. "But we have our reputations to think about. We can't be parking and have the sheriff drive up. We'd probably end up on the front page of the newspaper."

"Good point," he said and her heart sank.

He rubbed his chin. "It's not an insurmountable issue."

"You have a solution?" She couldn't keep the eagerness from her tone.

"My father owns a whole lot of land. Land that contains various places a truck could park. The sheriff doesn't patrol there."

Adrianna forced a casual tone. "It's a nice night for a drive."

"That, too." His gaze searched her eyes. "Only if you're interested."

"I've always felt that I missed something important by not, uh, engaging in typical teenage rites of passage." Adrianna waved a casual hand, hoping he'd think her burning cheeks were from too much makeup. "So yes, I'm interested. Unless you think we're making a mistake."

He grinned. "Let's do it anyway."

CHAPTER TWELVE

If someone had asked Adrianna exactly where she and Tripp were headed on that clear star-filled night in September, she would have admitted she didn't have a clue.

Tripp kept the conversation light on their way out of town. They'd driven for about fifteen minutes when he turned off the highway in the direction of his parents' ranch. Instead of taking the lane leading to the house, he chose a side road she'd never noticed before.

Darkness surrounded them, creating an air of intimacy in the cab that Adrianna found both comforting and terrifying. "It sure is dark out here."

"I like it." A tiny smile played on the edges of Tripp's lips. "Other than my family, this feeling of being part of the land is what I missed most when I was gone."

"You're happy you came back." It was a statement, not a question.

"From the moment I left, I couldn't wait to return." He paused. "But life isn't always about what just one person wants."

Even though he didn't mention Gayle's name, Adrianna knew that was whom he'd meant. Her friend had discovered she loved big-city life and would have never willingly moved back to Jackson Hole.

"How about you?" he asked. "Are you happy here?"

Adrianna tried to relax against the back of the seat and not think of the reason they were making this late-night drive on a dark, deserted road. Not because she was dreading what she assumed would occur once the truck came to a stop, but because anticipation held her body in a fever grip.

"Very happy." Adrianna smiled. "To me, Jackson Hole is the most beautiful place on earth. I can't imagine living anywhere else."

Suddenly, unexpectedly, the truck pulled to a stop. Tripp cut the lights and complete darkness closed in around them.

The only sounds in the car were her rapid breaths. Tripp didn't respond to her comment, which told her the time for conversation was over.

There was no reason to be apprehensive, she told herself. After all, it wasn't as if she was some naive schoolgirl. "Because this is meant to be an educational experience, perhaps you could tell me what usually happens?"

"It varies," Tripp said, sounding surprisingly serious. "That's something we should discuss."

"Is there usually a formal discussion prior to the...kissing?" Even though she'd asked the question, Adrianna couldn't imagine two high school students having any sort of heavy-duty discussion. A nervous laugh escaped her lips. "I'm sorry. That was a stupid question."

"A discussion usually isn't necessary." Tripp gazed at her across the darkened interior. "When you're dating someone, you have a good idea of how far they're willing—or wanting—to go. The guy should respect those boundaries."

Adrianna gazed out the windshield at a sky filled with stars. There was an underlying question beneath his words that she had to address. "Well, we're definitely not going all the way."

Thankfully, he didn't act shocked by her bluntness. "Which is a good thing, because I don't have any condoms with me."

Adrianna inhaled sharply. The way he'd said it made it sound as if intercourse *would* have been an option otherwise.

"Kissing is on the table," he said.

She nodded.

"French-kissing?"

Could this get any more embarrassing? Adrianna kept her gaze focused on the stars, her heart fluttering. "That would be okay, too."

"How much further are you willing to go?"

Adrianna took a deep breath, her mind racing. She should shut this discussion down right now. Tell him that she'd made a mistake; that while she appreciated his going along with her fantasy, it was best that they head back into town.

But when she met his gaze and saw him looking at her with those eyes filled with desire, she couldn't resist the chance to know what making out with Tripp Randall would be like.

"I think we should simply decide at the time." There, that seemed to be a civilized response.

"Sounds like a rational approach." His fingers played with her hair.

"It'll probably be over pretty quickly anyway."

Surprise skittered across his face. "What makes you say that?"

Adrianna lightly tapped the gear shift protruding from the console between them. "Seems to me we've got a pretty effective chaperone."

"Oh, we're not going to make out here." Tripp chuckled. "Not enough room."

Puzzled, Adrianna frowned. "I thought that's why we drove up here."

"It's a beautiful night," he said with a boyish smile. "I thought we'd put a blanket in the truck bed and look at the stars."

Look at the stars? Well, she guessed that sounded better than "make out," which reminded her way too much of high school. Not that she'd made out with anyone back then. Unless you counted Darrell Hecker, who'd been in band with her and kissed her cheek one time after a swing concert.

"Okay." She reached for her door handle, thankful they'd gotten everything settled.

"Whoa." He touched her arm. "Wait. I'll open the door."

"I'm perfectly capable of opening my own door," she said stiffly.

He grinned. "I have no doubt of that, but let me be a gentleman for a few more seconds."

A shiver of anticipation skittered up her spine. Did that mean that he was thinking of not being a gentleman once they reached the truck bed? Would she get a teeny glimpse of Tripp's wild side tonight? She could only hope.

"Before we do this," she heard him say, "in order to fulfill your fantasy—for as long as we're here—we're going back to those high school days. For now, we're not Tripp the CEO or Adrianna the nurse midwife—we're just two high school kids parking."

Even though Adrianna had never been interested in acting and had never been particularly good at role-playing during those silly party games, she liked the idea of not being her adult self this evening. "I'll give it a try."

He smiled and something flickered in the back of his eyes. It told her that Tripp was as ready as she to shed his adult persona for some simple, wholesome fun.

She shifted in her seat, gripped by anticipation, while he got out, retrieved a red plaid blanket from the backseat and rounded the front of the truck.

When he opened the door and held out his hand, her teenage self hesitated.

"What's wrong?" he asked.

She batted her lashes at him. "If my parents knew I was up here alone with you, they'd have a fit."

He smiled, a cocky, confident grin you'd expect from a football hero and class president. "I've got a solution. Don't tell them."

Adrianna laughed and held out her hand. "I like the way you think."

"I like the way you taste," he said, taking her fingers in his. "I haven't been able to get that kiss out of my mind. All I can think about is you. And me. Together."

Her heart tripped over itself. "I haven't been able to stop thinking about it either."

"Is that why you agreed to come here with me?" he asked in a low tone, although there was no one around for miles. "Please tell me it wasn't to look at the stars."

"It was you." Her voice came out low and husky. "It's always been you."

He winked. "It's always been you, too, babe."

Even though he was just making stuff up as he went, Adrianna had spoken the truth. From the time she'd been a teenager, Tripp had mesmerized her. Perhaps tonight's brief interlude would help get him out from under her skin.

After lowering the end gate, he helped her climb into the back of the truck. She stood while he spread the blanket.

"You know," he said, "if we lie down, we'll have a great view of the stars."

"I think you have more in mind than looking at the stars, Tripp Randall." A sound burst forth from Adrianna's throat that could only be described as a giggle. It took her by such surprise that she giggled again.

"Perhaps I do." Tripp sat on the blanket and tugged her down next to him.

She heaved an exaggerated sigh. "I don't think my parents would approve of my sitting this close."

"True." He grinned. "Then again, they wouldn't approve of your being up here in the first place."

He took her hand, urging her even closer. Even though the

night breeze now held a hint of coolness, heat was rolling off Tripp Randall in waves and Adrianna was anything but cold.

When he put his arm around her shoulders, she gave in to desire and rested her head against his broad chest.

"This is nice," she said, her fingers playing with the buttons on his shirt. "I don't think either of us will be comfortable like this for long."

A smile played at the corners of his mouth. "If we lie down, we'll be out of the wind."

Adrianna convinced herself that lying beside Tripp would be the same as being on a giant beach towel next to a friend. Once she was next to him, she realized, this didn't have that crowded-beach feel.

Then he tugged her to him and kissed her. The touch of his lips sent tiny electrical currents racing through her body.

"You told me I was only a 'good' kisser," he murmured against her mouth.

Jeesh, did the guy have a memory like a steel trap or what?

"Give me a chance to change your opinion."

A shiver of excitement traveled up Adrianna's spine. "Tell me we're not going to spend all night talking."

Almost immediately his lips closed over hers once again. This kiss started out sweet and gentle but quickly escalated into something deliciously dangerous.

When his tongue swept across her lips, she slipped her fingers into his silky hair and opened her mouth to him. The thought of having even a small part of him inside her was incredibly erotic.

Her breasts tingled and an ache began between her legs. By the time they came up for air, Adrianna was breathing hard and a delightful shiver of wanting filled her body.

Tripp trailed a finger down her cheek. "Was that more to your liking?"

She couldn't stop the smile from lifting her lips. "You're definitely on the right track."

"Hmm." His gaze dropped to her chest, lingering on her breasts straining against the fabric. "Let me try again."

"If you want." She tried to force a bored tone, but the words sounded more breathless than bored.

The kisses began again. Slow, leisurely ones that stoked the fire burning inside her. The flames were on the verge of an inferno when he eased the zipper down on her dress and slipped the fabric from her shoulders.

"What are you doing?" she asked in that still-oddly-breathless tone, arching her neck back as he nibbled on her ear.

"Making it a little more convenient."

"Convenient?" She inhaled sharply as his fingers unhooked her strapless bra, and suddenly she was naked from the waist up.

"For me to do this." His mouth closed over one sensitive nipple, while his fingers teased the tip of the other one.

"I'm sure my parents wouldn't approve of this," she panted.

He lifted his head from her breast, the tip still wet from his mouth. "Do you want me to stop?"

"Don't you dare." Her breath came in little puffs.

He chuckled before kissing her with such heat that she feared she would self-combust. Then he returned to her breasts. Her senses remained on overload as he nipped, sucked and licked, then trailed his tongue down her belly. At the same time his hand slipped up and under her dress.

He cupped her and she squirmed, pressing against his hand, wanting to prolong the sensations flooding her body.

Still, some sanity remained.

"I'm not going all the way with you," she panted, though that was exactly what she wanted to do. Give him her body as she'd already given him her heart.

"I know," he said in a tense voice. "That doesn't mean I can't bring you pleasure."

Before his words could even register, he pushed aside her panties and slipped two fingers inside her. She bucked upward, her muscles clenching tightly against him as he slowly began moving his fingers in and out. In and out. At that moment she'd have done anything, given him anything he asked.

"You're so wet." He nuzzled her breast as his fingers continued to work their magic.

In and out. In and out. The pressure began to build.

When his mouth closed over her breast and he began to suckle, Adrianna could no longer hold it in.

She cried out and arched back as a climax ripped through her, riding wave after wave of pleasure. He kept his fingers inside her until she shuddered.

Then he pulled back, gently pulling her dress down from where it was bunched around her waist to cover her thighs. Even though her bra was not in ready reach, she lifted the top of her dress over her breasts with shaking hands.

"I don't know what just happened there." Her voice shook. "But you definitely jumped into the 'great' range."

He chuckled and she felt some of the embarrassed tension leave her. While she'd just had the ride of her life, it had all been for her pleasure. Surely this situation fell under "do unto others as you would have them do unto you."

Adrianna closed her hand around the bulge in his jeans and felt his erection jump. "Can I reciprocate?"

His eyes met hers.

"I want to," she said, her voice trembling slightly. "I really do."

"Let me take a rain check," he said, kissing her firmly one last time. "It's late."

There'd been intimacy in the darkness, as if no one in the world existed but the two of them. But when he retrieved her panties, which had been slung over the edge of the truck bed, reality returned. Adrianna was forced to admit she'd lost control.

There wasn't much conversation as she adjusted her clothes and pulled on her panties. Her hands shook and she fumbled with her zipper. Tripp stepped close, zipping her up with well-practiced ease, stopping only to press a kiss against the back of her neck.

Even after they were back in the cab of the truck and headed home, Adrianna's engine still raced. Sex, she realized, could be addictive.

"It was lucky I didn't date much in high school," Adrianna said with a strained laugh as Tripp flicked on the headlights and started down the road.

He cast a curious sideways glance.

"I think I'd have had trouble keeping my panties on."

"The situation got out of hand tonight," he muttered. "I let it get out of hand."

For a second she didn't understand what he was saying. Then she realized he feared he'd overstepped. "I liked every bit of what you did."

His lips pressed together. "This was supposed to be a simple make-out session."

She lifted a shoulder in a slight shrug, feeling remarkably mellow. "It didn't get *that* far out of hand. We stayed on second base."

Tripp raked a hand through his hair. "We can't do this again."

She gave a throaty chuckle. "Now you sound like a parent."

"I'm serious, Adrianna."

"If you don't want to do it again, we won't," she said in a matter-of-fact tone.

"Now you're talking sense."

"But it's too bad." She gave him a Madonna-like smile. "I was ready to steal third base."

CHAPTER THIRTEEN

Adrianna climbed the steps of the church to the sound of the opening hymn. She didn't always attend, but Betsy had left a message last night informing her that today Nate would be wearing the little sailor outfit she'd given him.

She stopped in the back of the church and looked for Betsy and Ryan but didn't see them. The only empty seats she could see from where she stood were in the very back row, the one usually reserved for parents with little ones.

Then, Hailey Randall turned and motioned her forward. Adrianna smiled and hurried down the aisle as the congregation stowed their hymnals and began to sit.

She'd thought Hailey was alone. A tall couple in the seats behind the girl had blocked her view of Tripp's parents...and of Tripp.

His eyes widened when she slid into the pew next to his sister.

Tripp's mother smiled, her eyes lighting at the sight of Adrianna. "Hailey," she said to her daughter in a low tone, "move over so Adrianna can sit next to Tripp."

"Not necess—" Adrianna began, but stopped when she realized it wasn't going to make a difference.

Thankfully, the seat exchange didn't take long and she was soon ensconced between Tripp's father and the man who'd taken her to the moon and back last night.

"Hi," she whispered, heat coloring her cheeks.

Tripp smiled easily, but she saw the worry in his eyes. She wished they were alone and she could reassure him that even in the light of day, nothing had changed. She still didn't regret what had happened last night. And there had been an extra benefit. Although she'd recently been struggling with insomnia, last night she'd slept like a baby.

Perhaps she should tell her family-practice doc to prescribe orgasms for his insomniac patients. The thought of saying that to old Dr. Powell brought a smile to her lips.

"What's so funny?" Tripp whispered.

"I'll tell you later," she said and refocused on the Bible readings.

By the time the minister stood up to deliver the sermon, Adrianna realized that sitting next to Tripp had been a mistake. Not a little mistake. A big one.

Her body recognized him as last night's purveyor of pleasure. And it wanted to play some more. The pressure of his thigh against her legs sent fire shooting through her limbs. The intoxicating scent of his cologne brought back memories of his lips nuzzling her breast.

Without warning an ache began between her legs and her breasts strained against the front of her shirtdress, yearning for his touch.

"Stop it," she muttered.

"Did you say something?" Tripp leaned closer and the clean, fresh scent of him washed over her.

She inhaled deeply, which made her body shudder with pent-up need. Who knew the smell of soap had aphrodisiac properties?

"Adrianna?" Tripp whispered.

"I'm fine," Adrianna managed to sputter, keeping her eyes focused straight ahead. Having this type of reaction in a house of worship, well, it didn't get much worse.

I'm probably going to hell, she thought. She had to get her mind off Tripp and onto something else.

When listening to the sermon didn't work, she began counting sheep. One, two, three... She'd reached three hundred and sixty-five by the time the minister finished and they rose for the next hymn.

Then Tripp held out the hymnal and his hand brushed hers. The memories started up all over again. The touch of his hand on her breast, the way his fingers had moved in...

No, she absolutely would not go there.

She took the church bulletin and fanned herself, singing the words to the hymn with extra gusto.

Normally the fifty-minute service zoomed by. Today it dragged. By the time it concluded, Adrianna felt as though she'd swum through shark-infested waters and barely made it out alive.

"Adrianna," Tripp's dad said with a welcoming smile, "I'm so glad you could join us this morning. Tripp didn't tell us you were coming."

"I, uh, wasn't sure I'd be able to make it," she said, which was the truth. She was thankful she didn't have to add another lie to her list of sins.

"Are you going out for breakfast with your group of friends?" Kathy asked.

Adrianna slanted a sideways glance at Tripp. "I, uh, think so. Ryan and Betsy brought the baby and—"

Before she could ramble any more, Tripp stepped in. "We're headed over to The Coffeepot right now."

A look of relief crossed his mother's face. All Adrianna could figure was that she'd picked up on the tension between them and misunderstood. "Well, we won't keep you. Stop out at the house today if you get the chance. We'd love to see you."

"Mom," Tripp pointed out, "we just had dinner with you Friday night."

"I know," his mom said, looking straight at Adrianna, "but we loved seeing you."

"I enjoy visiting with you, too," Adrianna said.

As they walked down the aisle of the church and out into the bright sunshine, Tripp placed his hand against the small of Adrianna's back.

She inhaled sharply.

He let his hand fall to his side, but as they headed to their vehicles, he pulled her aside, a look of concern in his eyes. "Is everything okay?"

Other than I'm about to self-combust? She smiled. *"Everything is fine."*

"I don't think it is," he persisted. The look of dogged determination on his face told her he wouldn't let up until she spilled her guts. "You flinch each time I touch you. Why?"

"It's not what you think."

"Then tell me what it is."

"You unearthed a simmering volcano."

Tripp's brows pulled together in confusion. "I did—"

He stopped and she saw the instant he realized what she'd just said. For a second, a pleased look filled his eyes before disappearing. "I got you all hot and bothered."

"The minister was talking and all I could think about was what you could do with those lips." She lowered her voice. "And fingers."

That gorgeous—and talented—mouth quirked upward in a boyish grin. "You liked it, huh?"

"You were—"

"If you say 'good,' I'm going to have to kiss you."

She laughed aloud, causing several people walking by to turn and smile. "You were magnificent. I tried to tell you last night. I don't think you heard me."

His eyes grew serious. "I stand by what I said. I think it's best for both of us if we, uh, don't indulge again."

"With you."

"What did you say?"

"You think it's best that I don't indulge again with you."

"Who else would there be? We're dating."

"In a manner of speaking, yes."

"We're exclusive." His blue eyes bored into hers, challenging her to disagree.

"You're right. For the next few weeks that's true," she acknowledged. "After that..."

"After that, what?" He took a step closer, a belligerent look in his eye.

"We'll be free to do whatever we want." She smiled and brushed a strand of hair back from her face, a gesture that seemed oddly sensual. "With each other. Or with whomever we choose."

Tripp found himself more disturbed by her words than he let on. Was Adrianna really saying that she planned to sleep around once they broke up?

Of course, they wouldn't really be breaking up because they'd never been together in the first place.

It sure felt as if you were with her last night.

He pulled into a parking space not far from The Coffeepot and slammed his door with extra force. To top it off, she'd refused to ride to the café with him.

After dropping her bombshell, she'd offered up some lame excuse about needing to run to the grocery store after breakfast. He snorted.

Could the day get any worse?

"Randall, I didn't expect to see you here this morning. I thought you'd be in church."

Tripp turned to find Winn Ferris stepping onto the sidewalk from the curb. Yep, he decided, the day not only *could* get worse, it just had.

"Church just got out." Tripp saw the red of Adrianna's dress disappearing into the popular downtown café. He picked up his pace.

"Are you having breakfast at The Coffeepot?" Winn said with an easy smile. "I'm headed there myself."

"Yes." Tripp clipped the word. "I'm meeting some friends and I'm late. If you'll excuse me—"

"Well, look at this," Nick Delacourt said, approaching from the opposite direction with his wife, Lexi.

Tripp wasn't sure if Nick meant seeing Winn or seeing the two of them together. He didn't care to find out. He increased his pace, wanting to make sure he got a seat next to Adrianna.

"Are you meeting anyone for breakfast?" Lexi asked Winn.

"No." Winn gave a little laugh. "I just got tired of my own cooking and decided to check out this place."

"You're welcome to join us," Nick offered. "We have a large table toward the back. Who comes varies from week to week."

"I'd like that." Winn cast a pointed glance at Tripp, as if reminding him that he should have been the one to offer the invitation. "It'll be my chance to get to know everyone a little better."

Great, Tripp thought, *just great.* The day was getting better by the second.

The only good point was when he reached the table, Adrianna smiled at him and patted the chair next to where she was sitting. "I saved you a seat."

Feeling oddly triumphant, Tripp pulled the chair back. He hoped Winn would take the empty seat at the far end of the table.

Instead he chose the one next to Mitzi Sanchez, right across the table from Adrianna.

"I haven't seen you in a while," Tripp said to Mitzi.

Mitzi was an orthopedic surgeon who'd moved to Jackson Hole after residency. Some had linked her with Benedict Campbell, another physician in her group, but their relationship—if you could even call it that—had been tumultuous from the beginning.

Mitzi's lips lifted in a wry smile and Tripp realized for not the first time that she was a beautiful woman. With her blue eyes and brownish-red hair, she looked more Irish than Argentinean. Even though Tripp liked her personally, for some reason he'd never been attracted to her. "You'd think with the ski season over we wouldn't be as busy. But car accidents and trampolines have kept the surgery schedules full."

"Is Ben here with you?"

Mitzi rolled her eyes. "I don't know why everyone keeps asking me about him. We're colleagues. Sometimes we're even friends. But we're certainly not joined at the hip."

"On that positive note—" Winn smiled broadly and held out his hand to her "—I'm Winn Ferris and I'm not joined to anyone's hip either."

Tripp expelled a breath of relief, then turned to Adrianna, who looked positively lovely in bright red. The only thing he didn't like about her dress was it didn't show much skin. On second thought, with Winn at the table, that was a good thing.

"Thanks for saving me a seat," he said in a low tone.

She gave him a wink. "That's what girlfriends do."

"Were you and Tripp at the movies last night?" Kate asked. Kate was a pediatrician in town and married to Joel Dennes, a prominent builder of high-end homes. "Joel and I had a date night and he swore he saw you and Tripp come in."

Tripp glanced at Joel, a warning in his gaze. "We were there."

If Joel had seen anything...unusual, he'd best keep it to himself.

The builder simply smiled benignly and took a sip of coffee.

"I absolutely loved the movie." Kate shifted her gaze to Adrianna. "Tell me honestly, didn't you feel like crying when they broke up?"

"I'm not much of a crier," Adrianna admitted. "But I love it when good acting makes you feel such intense emotions."

Good save, Tripp thought to himself. Adrianna hadn't really said she'd watched the scene, but somehow she'd managed to answer Kate's question. He was glad no one had asked him anything about the movie because he'd been otherwise occupied.

When the older waitress with garish orange lipstick approached the table and began taking orders, Adrianna leaned toward Tripp.

"I hope everything is okay with Betsy and the baby." Her brows were furrowed with worry. "She'd told me she and Ryan would be in church, but I didn't see them."

Impulsively he reached over and gave her hand a squeeze. "I'm sure they're fine. Perhaps they just decided to sleep in."

"Oh, my goodness, it's Betsy and Ryan," Lexi called out.

Adrianna turned, her eyes lighting with pleasure. "And baby Nathan."

"We can make more room at the table." Nick started to rise to his feet.

"Don't bother." Ryan waved him down. "We can stay for only a second. We don't want the baby out around many people when he's so small."

"I wanted to show everyone how cute he looks in the outfit Adrianna gave him." Betsy held out the baby boy, dressed in a blue-and-white sailor suit, to her friend.

Adrianna took him in her arms with well-practiced ease. "He's adorable, Bets. The sailor hat is so cute on him."

"You should take a picture of him wearing it," Tripp said in a low tone to Ryan. "You can show it to his rodeo buddies when he's sixteen and they come over to the house."

"Betsy loves it on him," he said, looking surprisingly serious. "That's what matters."

"She's got you whipped, boy," Tripp teased.

"Guilty," Ryan said with an easy smile. He lowered his voice. "Seriously, I've never been happier. I can't believe it took me so long to see Betsy was the woman for me."

The waitress gave up on taking orders for the moment as the women congregated around Betsy and the baby.

Ryan and Tripp took a step back.

"I hear you and Adrianna are...involved."

Tripp wondered if Adrianna had told Betsy the truth about their relationship yet. If so, what had Betsy told Ryan?

"I'm happy to see you two together," Ryan continued, not waiting for Tripp to respond. "I thought you'd be perfect for each other for a long time."

A long time? Tripp had been with Gayle for years. Was his friend intimating...?

"Adrianna wasn't even on my radar when I was married," Tripp said abruptly.

"Of course not," Ryan said, a look of surprise in his eyes. "I know you were faithful to Gayle. I was just saying that Adrianna seems happy."

Tripp glanced at the midwife holding the tiny baby, who was gripping her finger with his little hand. Ryan was right. She did look happy. Perhaps this one-month fake relationship hadn't been such a bad idea after all.

The baby unexpectedly let out a mewing cry that reminded Tripp of one of the ranch kittens.

"Time to head home," Betsy said with an apologetic smile.

Adrianna handed the baby back to Betsy with apparent reluctance. "He's gorgeous, Bets. Simply gorgeous."

"We think he's pretty special," her friend said with a proud smile.

After more hugs and handshakes, the couple left and everyone returned to their seats. The waitress finished taking their orders and the topic turned to Travis and Mary Karen's retro party next weekend.

"Tell me we're not going to have to play any silly games," Tripp said to Travis, who sat at the far end of the table.

The popular ob-gyn physician just smiled.

His wife, Mary Karen, was more direct. "Depends on what you consider silly, Mr. Randall. I'd think you'd enjoy the chance to play, say, Twister or spin the bottle with your beautiful girlfriend."

Girlfriend.

The charade had been a success. Everyone viewed them as a couple now. Tripp admitted it had been fairly easy for him to slip into that role. Too easy.

It's just a game, he told himself. No harm. No foul.

With everyone gazing at him so expectantly, he took Adrianna's hand in his and brought it to his lips. "You're right. Count me in on the game playing."

Some of the pleasure that had lit Adrianna's eyes dimmed and he realized how she'd taken his words.

He leaned close, brushing her cheek with his lips. "I'm looking forward to Saturday night."

"You're not the only one, Randall," Winn said, which told him the man had already secured an invitation. His gaze shifted and lingered on Adrianna. "I love Twister. And spin the bottle."

Tripp turned and met Winn's gaze head-on. Even though a smile remained on his lips, the look he shot Winn warned him to back off.

There was a responding challenge in Winn's eyes. One that told Tripp if he didn't keep Adrianna happy, Winn would.

Tripp placed his arm around the back of Adrianna's chair. Although he'd planned to catch up on some work this afternoon, it suddenly seemed prudent to spend time with the woman at his side. "Interested in doing some hiking this afternoon?"

A doubtful look filled Adrianna's emerald eyes. "Hiking?"

"Nothing too strenuous," he said. "I thought we could go to Yellowstone, walk around Jenny Lake, then have an early dinner at the lodge."

"I'm not much of an outdoorsy gal," Adrianna said slowly.

He smiled as an image of the two of them under the stars flashed before him.

"Oh, I think you're more outdoorsy than you think." His tone took on a seductive edge. "Give it a try. It'll be fun."

When she nodded and smiled, a surge of triumph raced through him. He told himself he was excited because he hadn't taken time to do much hiking this year. The truth was, he looked forward to spending the afternoon with Adrianna.

Far, far more than he should.

CHAPTER FOURTEEN

Adrianna glanced down at her green walking shorts and hiking shoes. Or she supposed they were hiking shoes. Because she'd never done any hiking, she wasn't sure what one wore for a walk around a lake. She'd picked the ugliest and most comfortable shoes in her closet.

She knew she couldn't wear a dress, although she had some pretty ones in her closet that Tripp hadn't yet seen. Instead she'd topped the shorts with a stretchy gold T-shirt and a plaid shirt in fall colors that she left hanging open.

Even though she thought she looked way too casual, the way Tripp smiled when he saw her seemed to indicate he liked the outfit. His cargo shorts and navy T-shirt weren't anything special, yet her gaze couldn't help lingering on his muscular legs and broad shoulders. She could honestly say that in all the years she'd lived in Jackson Hole, the hospital had never had such a good-looking CEO.

She'd worried she might feel awkward or be consumed with lust—like she had in church—when they were in the close confines of his truck. Thankfully, neither happened on the drive to Yellowstone.

Oh, she had to admit that her body still perked up when she was close to Tripp, and for a few minutes she couldn't help focusing on his lips. She hoped he didn't notice. Or if he did, he thought she was simply hanging on to his every word.

Honestly, she enjoyed their conversation. He talked about his studies at Yale and his time working for a large health system in NYC. She told him about her nursing education and how she'd decided she wanted to become a midwife after a stint in Labor and Delivery.

The only thing that disturbed her was Tripp seemed to be making a conscious effort to avoid mentioning Gayle. Adrianna thought about bringing her up. After all, she didn't want him to think he couldn't mention his own wife when he was with her, but the time never seemed right.

All too soon, they were at the park and out of the truck, ready to face the great outdoors. She shivered with sudden alarm.

Didn't snakes hang out by water?

"Have you ever been serious about a guy?" Tripp asked, after they'd started on the path around the large lake with the shimmering blue water.

Adrianna was so focused on scouting for reptiles slithering on the uneven terrain that the question didn't register at first. "What?"

"You're a beautiful, intelligent woman, Adrianna. I can't believe you've made it to almost thirty without being in a relationship."

"As you know, my parents were older and a bit overprotective." Saying the words felt wrong, as if she was dissing her mom and dad, which she wasn't. "I didn't date at all in high school."

"High school was a long time ago for both of us."

"Yes, I suppose you're right," she said, wondering why those years often loomed so large in her mind.

"What about college?" Tripp prompted.

Adrianna had tried to purge that time from her head. Especially the scandal that had erupted her senior year.

"I had a somewhat serious boyfriend," she said in what she hoped was a casual tone.

"You obviously didn't stay together."

Adrianna realized with a start that he'd taken her hand in an almost comforting gesture. With him beside her the sick feeling she got when she thought back to her college days didn't seem quite so pronounced. Or maybe the bad memories were finally beginning to fade. After all, that, too, had been such a long time ago.

"What happened?" Tripp prompted.

"Matt had a Jekyll-and-Hyde thing going." Adrianna tried to keep any bitterness from her voice. She thought she'd succeeded until Tripp gave her hand a squeeze and slanted a questioning look in her direction.

"At first he was sweet," she said with a sigh. "Then everything changed."

"What happened?"

His curiosity told her Gayle had kept the story to herself, as she'd requested. Betsy knew the truth, too. They were the only ones she'd told.

An air of watchful waiting hung heavily between them.

Before answering, Adrianna lifted her face to the sun and let the warmth seep into the deepest recesses of her soul. Even though she hadn't thought she'd ever tell him about that time, Adrianna suddenly wanted to explain. *Needed* to explain.

She felt close to Tripp. And she didn't like having secrets from someone she lo—well, from someone she considered a dear friend. Adrianna knew the risk she'd be taking in coming clean. He might listen to her story, then walk away in disgust. It would be worse to see the disappointment in his eyes.

Yet, she would tell him. Soon. Before she lost her nerve. They reached a clearing. After scanning the ground, Adrianna stepped close to shore. She stared out over the endless blue but found no pleasure in the beauty surrounding her.

"You don't have to tell me." Tripp moved behind her, wrapping his arms lightly around her waist.

She leaned back against his broad chest, drawing strength from his warmth. "Matt was a physics major," she began haltingly after several more seconds had passed. "I had a part-time position working for several professors in that department. That's how we met."

She tried to picture him in her mind, but after all these years the best she could come up with was a mass of rumpled dark hair and intense blue eyes. "I'd gone out with other guys, but after a couple of dates, I'd always lose interest."

"He was different," Tripp said against her hair, his voice giving nothing away.

"I think that was part of the appeal." Adrianna pulled her brows together. "He was so into me. I was flattered by the attention. No one had given me that much notice before. He was brilliant and handsome and he wanted *me*."

Tripp's only response was to stroke her arm.

"While all the attention he gave me was really great, it was also overwhelming at times. And a little...scary."

Tripp's hand halted midstroke.

"We were always together. My college girlfriends had quit calling. He didn't like my hanging around with them anyway." Adrianna's tone turned wistful. "I didn't have any family. With my oldest and dearest friends far away, there was just...him."

Tripp remained silent, allowing her to continue at her own pace.

"He had a temper. He'd get so angry with my *stupidity*, as he called it." Adrianna sighed. It had taken several years of therapy for her to understand why Matt had been so successful in dismantling her self-confidence.

Adrianna felt Tripp's body tense. She didn't wait for him to respond. "Midway through second semester Matt told me there was something I needed to do for him. Didn't ask. Told me."

"What did he want you to do?" Tripp's voice was tight with control.

"Nothing big." Adrianna gave a humorless laugh. "Just get him a copy of an upcoming midterm exam off his professor's computer. Matt wasn't as smart as I thought, because he was only pulling a B in that course. Such a low grade in his major could have impacted his choice of graduate programs."

"What did you tell him?"

Had Tripp asked, or had she just imagined the words?

"I said no. He was shocked. He tried everything to change my mind...including getting physical." She brought a hand to her cheek. While Adrianna may have blocked out Matt's facial features, she could still feel the sting of the hard slap that had turned the whole side of her face numb.

"He hit you?" Tripp's voice shook with a fury that made the leaves on the nearby trees quiver.

Adrianna gave a jerky nod. "Thankfully, one of his roommates came home just then and I ran out the door."

"Did he come after you?" Tripp's hands tightened around her arms.

She gave a little squeak. "Tripp, you're hurting me."

"Oh, sorry." He immediately loosened his hold and expelled a harsh breath. "That bastard should be—"

"Anyway." Even though this was ancient history, the rapid pounding of Adrianna's heart made it feel as though it had happened yesterday. She licked her dry lips. "I spent the night with a fellow nursing student. He called my cell thirty-two times. I didn't answer. The next day he came to the physics department where I was working. He had a bouquet of flowers and was all apologetic and contrite."

"I hope you told him what he could do with those flowers."

"I—I was confused." Adrianna closed her eyes and expelled a shuddering breath. "Remember, he was my life. Or so it seemed."

"Oh, Adrianna."

Her knees went weak at the caring in his voice. But her relief was tempered by the knowledge he still didn't know the full story.

Adrianna drew a deep breath, determined to press through to the end. "Shortly after Matt arrived, I took a call for one of the professors. The young man—who I learned later was Matt's friend—said it was crucial he speak with Dr. Douglass as soon as possible. He said he'd tried everything to reach him. I told the guy I could leave a message on the professor's door so he'd see it the instant he got out of class and returned to the office. Matt said he'd wait. By the time I got back he was gone."

"Good riddance," Tripp muttered.

"I settled back to work and immediately noticed someone had messed with my computer," she continued, ignoring his comment. "I worried Matt had gotten the test after all."

"Wasn't your PC password-protected?"

She nodded miserably. "He knew my password. We'd joked about the silly one I'd chosen months earlier. My suspicions were confirmed when a cheating scandal erupted."

Her eyes grew hot. Without another word, Adrianna pulled herself from Tripp's arms. She returned to the path that encircled the lake and began to walk. Adrianna had thought she'd made peace with that time in her life, but the surge of emotion fueling her steps told a different story. Angrily, she brushed unwanted moisture from her eyes.

"Adrianna." In several long strides, Tripp reached her.

When she turned and he saw the tears, he pulled her to him and hugged her. "It's okay, sweetheart. It's all good."

Adrianna's heart lodged in her throat. Tripp hadn't called her sweetheart since the night they'd informed everyone they were "a couple." But that had been part of the charade. This felt *real*.

"Matt and several others were kicked out of school." Adrianna sniffled and swiped at her eyes, determined to regain control. "Administration determined a group of students had gotten their hands on the test. They suspected it was through me, but couldn't prove it. Still, I lost my job. Being fired was...humiliating. I saw the look of derision in the dean's eyes, heard the disappointment in his voice." She shuddered.

His gaze searched hers. "Did you tell them what you suspected?"

She shook her head. "I was afraid I'd get kicked out, too."

"Why?"

"I'd given Matt my confidential password," she reminded him. "I'd left him alone in the office, giving him the opportunity."

"You couldn't have known he'd do something like that—"

"Couldn't I?" She breathed the last of her secrets, the one that had niggled at her for years. "Perhaps I secretly wanted to give him access. That way I could make him happy without being directly involved."

"No." Tripp's response was swift and sure. "That's not what happened."

"How can you be so certain?"

"Because I know you."

She shrugged.

"What were you feeling that morning?" Tripp asked. "When you saw...him?"

It was as if Tripp couldn't even bring himself to say Matt's name.

Adrianna thought for a moment. "Anger. Sadness."

"Did the flowers soften you up?"

"A little," she admitted, wanting to be completely honest. "I'd never gotten flowers before. He insisted he hadn't meant to hurt me, that his hand had...slipped."

"Slipped, my ass." A muscle in Tripp's jaw jumped. "Did any of it change your decision about helping him?"

"No," she said firmly.

"Would you have left him alone in the office if you'd known what he had planned?"

Adrianna shook her head.

"There's your answer, then," he told her.

"Maybe deep down—"

"Adrianna, no. Don't torment yourself over this. It was a long time ago and it's over." His lips curved up in a gentle smile. "Even if you *had* helped him, we all make mistakes. We learn from them and move on."

"You don't hate me?"

"I could never hate you." He trailed a finger down her cheek, then kissed her lightly on the lips.

The truth will set you free.

The doubts that had dogged Adrianna for many years slipped away in a rush of emotion. She lifted her face, wishing Tripp would kiss her again. Instead he took her hand and they began to walk.

After a couple of minutes of silence, he slanted a sideways glance. "Was there anyone after college?"

You, she wanted to say. Instead she lifted a shoulder in a slight shrug. "Work has always kept me busy...."

She let her voice trail off. She'd dated, but no one who touched her heart. That was, until she'd contacted Tripp a couple of months after Gayle had died. It had been a courtesy text, to show support and see how he was holding up. To her surprise, slowly and a bit awkwardly, an online friendship had ensued.

They'd grown close, via texts sharing thoughts and feelings that would be impossible to say in person. She'd had high hopes when Tripp had moved back to Jackson Hole. But from the second he arrived, he'd taken a step back from her. That was, until he'd approached her with this one-month-relationship idea.

"Have you dated anyone seriously since Gayle died?" she found herself asking. Even though he'd shared a lot via text messages, she wasn't foolish enough to assume he'd told her *everything*.

"Not really." His eyes were focused on the distant mountain peaks rather than on her. "I probably should jump back into the dating pool, but right now I don't have the time."

"You have time to see me," she pointed out.

"Yes," he finally said. "But we're not trying to build a relationship."

His words were like a hard punch, a blunt reminder that no matter how close she felt to him, no matter how many times he called her "sweetheart," he wasn't envisioning a future with her.

Even though Adrianna had tried to guard her heart, she now conceded she'd failed miserably. Perhaps she should call off this fake relationship right now. The second the thought crossed her mind, she cast it aside.

How could she walk away from Tripp now? And why? Whether their "relationship" ended today or in several weeks, she'd still be devastated.

"Carpe diem," she murmured.

When Tripp nodded, Adrianna realized with a start she must have spoken aloud.

"Seize the day." He shot her a wink. "That's exactly what we've been doing this past month."

The last thing she wanted to do was to continue talking about the relationship-that-wasn't, so Adrianna made a great show of taking in the serene alpine beauty surrounding them.

"I never would have gone hiking if you hadn't asked." She inhaled the fresh mountain air. "I'd have missed all this."

Adrianna gestured with her free hand toward the endless blue of lake, somehow encompassing Tripp in the gesture. Her skin prickled beneath his intense stare.

When their eyes locked, she inhaled sharply at the connection. It was as if she'd been transported back to when she was fourteen.

Adrianna remembered the day. She'd been carrying branches to the street for the garbageman. Seventeen-year-old Tripp had arrived to pick up Gayle. When he'd seen her stumbling to the curb, her arms overflowing with brush, he'd hurried over to help.

As he'd taken the branches from her arms, their eyes had met. She still remembered the jolt of awareness. She'd stood there in the hot sun, frozen for a heartbeat, maybe two, staring into his eyes. Her well-ordered world had tilted on its axis. That was the day she'd fallen in love.

For a second she was certain he'd experienced the same jolt. But then, like now, he'd blinked, then grinned.

"There's so much I want to show you," he said as they resumed walking.

Okay, so maybe this dating charade could be a learning experience for both of them. She could broaden her horizons and he could...

Well, there was no way she was going to be happy about watching Tripp swim off after being the one to ease him back into the dating pool. Still, she didn't have much choice. It was either seize the remaining days or walk away now.

For now, carpe diem would be her mantra.

Regrets, well, they could wait for another day.

CHAPTER FIFTEEN

By the time they walked around the entire lake and enjoyed a leisurely early dinner, Tripp decided this would be a good opportunity to lighten the mood by sharing his love of fishing with Adrianna.

Yet, when he told her he'd bought her a permit at the lodge and suggested they head over to Yellowstone Lake to see what they could catch, she looked at him as if he'd lost his mind.

That was when the excuses as to why it wouldn't work had started. He had an answer for each of her concerns. This morning he'd tossed a couple of fishing poles in the back of the truck, they had their permits and he had extra sunscreen in his tackle box.

When she finally admitted she was afraid of worms, he stifled a smile and promised to bait her hook. Soon they were basking in the sunshine, waiting for a fish or two to take the bait. He was glad he'd included a couple of lawn chairs because he had the feeling Adrianna wasn't quite ready to sit on a dusty bank.

The sun glimmered against the rich walnut strands of her hair. Her green eyes were covered with dark glasses and, because of the heat, she was down to shorts and a tiny T-shirt.

Even though she looked stunning, Tripp knew there was so much more to this woman than her beauty. She was intelligent and caring and she fit in well with his family. Earlier, when his eyes had locked with hers, he'd started rethinking what came next.

He could no longer deny that these past weeks had irrevocably changed things between them. To go back to simply being friends was impossible. But where to go from here was the burning question. Until he could sort things out, the intimacy they'd shared in that truck bed couldn't happen again. Regardless of the depths of his feelings for her, physically he must keep his distance.

Holding hands. A kiss or two. That was as far as it could go. He needed to make sure she understood that it wasn't that he didn't want her; he just had some hard thinking to do and needed a clear head.

A hastily constructed speech formed on Tripp's lips. He cleared his throat.

She lowered her glasses and peered at him, her eyes a vivid emerald-green.

"I have to touch you," he heard himself say as he reached over and took her hand.

A smile played at the corners of her lips. "Like last night."

Yes. *No.* It was time they speak about what had happened and what couldn't happen again. Not just yet anyway. Instead of immediately jumping into the speech, Tripp stroked her palm with his thumb. "I took it too far."

"You didn't do anything I didn't want you to do," she assured him in a soft voice.

"When we first discussed our...arrangement—" Tripp paused then began again "—something was said about keeping physical intimacy to a minimum."

Had he set that parameter? Or was that one of Adrianna's stipulations? Did it even matter?

Adrianna pulled her hand from his and stretched, her cotton shirt pulling tight across her chest. "That's the nice thing about verbal agreements."

With great effort, Tripp forced his gaze from her breasts, his mouth dry. "It is? I mean, what is?"

"They can be easily modified."

He swallowed. "Are you saying you want to modify our no-touching rule?"

She gave a throaty laugh that shot straight to his groin. "News flash. I think we already did."

Tripp couldn't stop himself from grinning.

"It's been a long time since I've been intimate with a man," Adrianna admitted, her cheeks pink from the sun. "Just as you're using our time together to get you ready to date, perhaps I can use the opportunity to jump back into the, well, the sexual side of things."

Tripp stilled. His smile vanished. Had she really just told him she would be using him for sex practice? His thoughts raced. Who would she be practicing for? A single name shot to the top of the list.

Winn Ferris.

He opened his mouth to tell her he didn't feel that was at all appropriate. Then it hit him what she was proposing wasn't really much different than his using her for dating practice.

Except that's not what I'm doing.

"I'm sorry," she said when the silence lengthened. "That didn't quite come out the way I intended. What I meant to say is there's no reason that our remaining time together can't be mutually advantageous."

Tripp knew most men would jump at this chance. He could practically guarantee that if she'd said these same words to Winn Ferris, he'd be on top of her by now.

But Tripp didn't want Adrianna for a couple more weeks; he wanted her—

"You remember what we decided will happen once the month is over," he heard her say.

"We'll remain friends," he said automatically, parroting their earlier agreement, "but go our separate ways."

"That was the deal," she said, an odd catch in her voice.

When Tripp lifted his gaze and stared into those beautiful emerald eyes, he realized he'd been a fool. Thirty days wasn't enough time with this woman.

It was time to renegotiate.

Despite their talk over fishing poles, once the week started there wasn't time for any sexual encounters with Tripp. Besides, Adrianna had just been jerking his chain about getting some experience. It had been a way of protecting her heart, of not wanting Tripp to see she'd fallen in love with him.

When he invited her to join him for dinner with his parents on Tuesday, she eagerly accepted. As always, the second she walked through the front door, a feeling of warmth and caring wrapped around Adrianna like a favorite sweater. She liked his father's gentle teasing and the way his mother's smile widened when she saw her. Lately, and for the first time since her parents had died, Adrianna felt part of a family.

Tripp's sister, Hailey, greeted her warmly as well. Prior to becoming "involved" with Tripp, all Adrianna knew about his sister was she was a speech pathologist who'd worked in Denver before returning to Jackson Hole. Hailey had mentioned she was hoping to get a position with the hospital or the school system, but so far nothing had come through.

Yesterday, while his sister had been at the hospital for a follow-up interview, she and Adrianna had met for a quick lunch in the cafeteria.

"You should have seen how Adrianna's eyes lit up when we

ran into Tripp," Hailey told her mother later when the men stepped outside for a second. "They had this cute little glow."

Adrianna gave a nervous laugh. "My eyes don't glow."

"Yes, they do," Hailey teased. "Tripp's eyes do the same thing when he sees you."

"I think it's sweet." Kathy handed Adrianna a cup of coffee with cream and sugar already added, just as she liked. "A woman should be happy to see someone she cares about."

It was obviously a case of people seeing what they wanted to see. At least Adrianna *hoped* she wasn't wearing her heart in her eyes. How embarrassing would that be?

Thankfully, Tripp and his father returned and over a delicious meal of veal parmigiana, the talk shifted to his mother's committee work and a change his father had recently instituted in his cattle-breeding program.

Throughout dinner, Adrianna caught Hailey and Kathy exchanging smiles whenever she looked in Tripp's direction. Even though she enjoyed the conversation, she was relieved when the meal ended. Once the table had been cleared and the dishwasher filled, Tripp asked if she wanted to sit outside with him.

"What a beautiful evening," Adrianna said, taking a seat on the wooden porch swing.

"You're beautiful." Tripp's arm slipped around her shoulders. "Inside and out."

"Thank you," she said in a light tone, trying to make sense of his behavior. Since their trip to Yellowstone on Sunday, she'd felt an increased closeness between them that she couldn't explain.

It was as if the wall that had loomed so large between them was crumbling. The way Tripp looked at her was now different. Perhaps his mother and sister had been right about the "glow."

"I like you, Adrianna," he said unexpectedly.

There had been no qualifier at the end. No *I like you...as a friend.* And the look in his eyes, well, it wasn't the kind you'd expect from a man who thought of you only as a buddy.

"I like you, too," she stammered.

Without warning she was in his arms and his warm, sweet lips were on hers. The kisses quickly grew more urgent. He was practically on top of her in the swing when the front screen door flew open.

"Oh." His mother blinked rapidly, her hand rising to her chest. "I didn't realize I was interrupting—"

Adrianna pushed Tripp off her and sat up, brushing her disheveled hair back from her face. The top button of her dress was unfastened. "We were just—"

"I know what you were doing, dear." Kathy offered Adrianna an understanding smile. "Frank and I have spent many a lovely evening doing the same thing on this swing."

"Where's Dad?" Tripp asked, trying to banish that image of his mom and dad from his brain.

"He wasn't feeling well, so he went to bed." A worried look crossed his mother's face before her smile returned. "He said to tell you both good-night."

"Please sit," Adrianna urged, patting a space next to her. "It's too beautiful a night to be inside."

His mother glanced questioningly in Tripp's direction. He shot her a reassuring smile. "Join us, Mother. There's plenty of room."

Even though Adrianna could be shy with strangers, Tripp had never seen her be that way with his parents. In fact, she talked easily with both his mom and dad, and seemed to revel in their attention.

He'd always wished Gayle and his mother had enjoyed a better relationship. His wife had been very close to her own mom and his mother's overtures had been often mistaken as getting into her business.

As Adrianna and his mother continued to talk, Tripp felt himself relax and his heart filled with hope.

Hope that he might finally be able to bury the guilt and embrace a real relationship with Adrianna.

Most of all, hope that this might be the beginning of something that would last a lifetime.

No charade.

No games.

Starting now.

～

The next day, jazzed after delivering a healthy baby girl to a couple who had struggled with infertility for years, Adrianna decided to stop by Tripp's office and see if he was free for lunch.

It's something a real girlfriend would do, she told herself, as she made her way down the shiny hallway toward the executive suites. She'd barely started out when she ran into Paula, Tripp's personal assistant, headed in the opposite direction.

They chatted for a few minutes before Paula glanced at her watch.

"Sorry to cut this short, Adrianna, but I'm meeting my sister for lunch."

Adrianna glanced in the direction of Tripp's office.

"He's just working on paperwork." Paula smiled. "I'm sure he'll welcome the interruption."

Adrianna was almost to the door of Tripp's office when she heard voices coming from inside and realized he wasn't alone. Someone must have stopped by after Paula left. Adrianna paused, unsure whether to knock or come back later.

"I'm sorry you didn't get the job, Hail," she heard Tripp say. "You'd have done a fabulous job."

"They hired someone with more experience," the female voice said, her words heavy with disappointment.

Adrianna immediately recognized Hailey's voice. Her heart sank. His sister was supposed to hear about the position at the hospital today. It appeared she'd heard and the news hadn't been good.

Knowing Hailey wouldn't mind the interruption, Adrianna put her hand on the doorknob. Her fingers froze in place when she heard her name.

"I adore Adrianna," Hailey said in a sweet, earnest voice. "I hope the two of you stay together."

Even though Adrianna strained to hear, his response was a low rumble she couldn't make out.

"Gayle is gone," Hailey replied in a firm tone. "This is now. I like Adrianna a whole lot more than I ever did her."

For a second Adrianna couldn't hear anything, but did she really need to listen any longer? It was obvious Tripp had told his little sister he was still desperately in love with Gayle. His next words confirmed that impression.

"Do you believe in soul mates?" This time Tripp's voice came through loud and clear.

Adrianna inhaled sharply. Turning quickly on her heel, she quietly slipped back into the hall where she paused, her heart thumping in her ears. After this weekend, she'd been hopeful things were changing between her and Tripp. It was as if they were standing on the verge of something spectacular. But the bit of conversation she'd just heard told her nothing had changed.

Tripp was still hung up on Gayle. Perhaps always would be. Even if she and Tripp got together, would Gayle always be number one in his heart?

More importantly, could Adrianna be content with being number two?

～

"I'm happy you stopped over." Betsy settled her infant son into the stroller. "And that the weather cooperated so we could take a walk."

"It seems like forever since I've seen you." Adrianna experienced a rush of emotion. She'd missed these chats with her friend. "You've been so busy with the baby—"

"And you've been so busy with Tripp," Betsy said with a sly smile, starting down the driveway, leaving Adrianna no choice but to follow. "Tell me, how's that going?"

"I love him, Betsy." The words slipped past her lips before she could stop them.

"I know." Betsy turned the stroller down the sidewalk.

"You know?"

Betsy chuckled. "It *is* rather obvious."

"Really?" That blasted light in her eyes had betrayed her again.

Betsy nodded and waved to an older couple walking on the sidewalk across the street. "I'm happy for you, Adrianna. I always thought you and Tripp would make a perfect couple."

"It's hard to compete with Gayle."

Surprise filled Betsy's eyes. "Gayle is his past. You're his future."

"She was perfect for him." Adrianna gave a heavy sigh. "They'd been together forever. They had all this shared history."

"One day you'll have decades of shared history together, too."

Adrianna thought for a moment. She supposed Betsy did have a point. "I want to be with him so much it scares me."

Betsy jiggled the carriage when the baby started to fuss. Once he quieted, she turned to her friend. "What frightens you?"

"That I won't be enough for him. Or that I'll always be second best. I think they were—" Adrianna swallowed hard "—soul mates."

The thought hurt far more than it should.

As expected, instead of tossing off some platitude as other

friends might, Betsy paused and met Adrianna's gaze. "Those are serious concerns."

Adrianna had given the matter a lot of thought. She'd tried to convince herself she could be happy with just a tiny portion of Tripp's heart, but she knew that wasn't true.

"I don't believe you'll be happy being second best," Betsy said softly.

The corners of Adrianna's lips dropped. "I won't."

"You need to speak with Tripp," Betsy urged. "Tell him your fears."

"I don't think I can." After all, Tripp hadn't even said he loved her. Or given any sign he wanted to be with her permanently. He certainly had no idea she'd overheard his private conversation with his sister.

"You say you love him?"

Adrianna nodded.

"The way I see it, if you're old enough to be in love with a man, to even consider a future with that man, you should be mature enough to talk to him about your feelings." Betsy slipped her arm through Adrianna's and gave it a squeeze. "Once you have all the facts, you can make your decision."

"Our thirty days will be up soon," Adrianna murmured, wondering why that was even relevant.

"I know you're feeling discouraged. I had some of those same fears when Ryan and I were dating," Betsy said with an understanding smile. "You know what I discovered?"

"What's that?"

"Sometimes we do get what we want." Betsy smiled at her son, then raised her gaze to meet Adrianna's. "I did. Something tells me you will, too."

CHAPTER SIXTEEN

Adrianna was fully prepared to confront Tripp about his feelings for her the next night. She planned to do it when they met for coffee after a chamber of commerce meeting they both planned to attend.

But one of her patients showed up in labor at the end of the workday, and she'd had to cancel. When she'd called Tripp, he said no worries, they'd be seeing each other the next night.

At first she thought he might have something special planned, but he'd simply told her his parents had insisted they come for dinner that night.

Even though she enjoyed seeing his parents, Adrianna admitted—but just to herself—that she wished Tripp had planned something special involving just the two of them. Most of all, she wished he'd remembered her birthday.

The staff at work had brought a cake. She'd received birthday cards in the mail from her friends. Tripp hadn't mentioned her big day once. Not when he'd called to make the "date." Not when he'd arrived at her place to pick her up with empty hands.

They were driving up the lane to his parents' home when she

decided she was being ridiculous. While he'd promised at the country club party to make a mental note of the date, everyone knew men were notoriously bad about remembering special occasions.

"Perhaps, on our way home tonight, we could stop at Hill of Beans and share a piece of cake," Adrianna said in what she hoped was an off-hand kind of tone. "Their triple chocolate is my favorite."

"I believe you mentioned that to me once," he said.

"Because today is my birthday," she said quickly, "and though I don't often eat sweets, I do like to have cake on special occasions."

"Your birthday?" He slanted a glance her way, not appearing overly impressed. "Well, happy birthday, Adrianna."

"Thanks." Her lips began to tremble and it was only with great effort that she managed to keep the smile on her lips.

You're not a child, she told herself sternly. Birthdays are just not that big of a deal to most people.

Still, she found herself dragging her feet as they parked, then headed up the walk to his parents' porch. She climbed the steps and suddenly made her decision. Once they reached the top step, she lightly touched Tripp's arm.

He tipped his head back and smiled.

"Do me a favor," she said, swallowing past the emotion clogging her throat. "Don't tell your parents it's my birthday."

Clearly puzzled, his brows pulled together. "Why not?"

"I don't want them to feel bad that they didn't make a fuss." Adrianna had gotten to know Tripp's mother well. Kathy would feel terrible that not only hadn't she realized it was Adrianna's birthday, but she also hadn't done anything special to help her celebrate.

Tripp shrugged and reached around her for the screen door.

"Tripp," she said, urgency in her voice, "promise me."

He pushed open the door and gestured for her to step inside.

"Tripp," she said again, not bothering to conceal her irritation at his lackadaisical attitude. Didn't he realize how bad his mother would feel? Kathy had enough on her mind without—

"Happy birthday!" The words rang out from dozens of voices followed by laughter. Then the singing began, an off-key rendition but with much gusto.

Adrianna widened her eyes, taking in the faces of friends and colleagues. Her heart skipped a beat. Then another. She smiled, a goofy grin that only got wider as the song progressed.

When the chorus ended, Tripp leaned close, kissed her cheek, then whispered, "Did you really think I'd forgotten your birthday?"

Tears of joy slipped down Adrianna's cheeks. She hastily wiped them away as her friends crowded around.

There were balloons everywhere and decorations celebrating the "Big 3-0." Frank and Kathy Randall stood back with huge smiles on their faces. Adrianna rushed over to them and gave them each a hug. "Thank you for remembering and doing all this."

"Thank my son," Kathy said proudly. "He orchestrated the whole thing, but we were very happy to help him put it together."

Adrianna's heart swelled with emotion as she made her way through the crowded room, accepting more birthday wishes.

There was a buffet table with all her favorite foods and a table full of presents. Looking around, Adrianna knew the greatest gifts weren't the ones in brightly colored wrapping paper and gauzy bows. The friendship of each and every person in the room this evening was what mattered most.

Tripp remained at her side the entire evening. When he brought in a triple-chocolate cake from Hill of Beans, decorated with thirty candles glowing brightly, Adrianna's heart burst with joy.

"Thank you so much, everyone," she said, but her eyes were

on him. On the man who had made this the best birthday ever. On the man she loved.

⁓

"I wanted to stay and help your mother clean up." Adrianna turned to face Tripp when they reached the front door of her condo.

"I heard you the first ten times." A smile tugged at the corners of his lips. "What was my response?"

"That she has Hailey tonight and the housekeeper tomorrow," she said a bit sulkily. "It was a fabulous party. I want her to know just how much I appreciate her going to all the effort—"

"She knows." He closed her lips with his fingers. "She's also aware that your special night is far from over."

Adrianna met his gaze and something in her belly clenched at the look in his eyes.

"I still have to give you my gift."

She couldn't stop herself. Her eyes, which seemed to suddenly develop a mind of their own, zeroed in on the area directly below his belt buckle.

Tripp chuckled, a low, pleasant rumbling sound. "Something in addition to that…"

Adrianna's heart did a backflip. Was he saying that tonight they would finally make love?

What about Gayle?

Even though the worry had consumed her waking hours for the past few days, she swept the thought aside as of no consequence. When she looked into Tripp's eyes tonight, what she saw there had reassured her that she was the one he wanted. Her. Only her.

Even if she was wrong, if she couldn't delude herself on her birthday, when could she?

"Aren't you going to invite me in?"

Adrianna turned toward him, her pulse rioting. "If you promise to behave yourself," she teased.

"I'm not making any such promise, darlin'." He bent his head and planted a hot kiss on the side of her neck. "I don't think you really want me to."

With heart pounding, Adrianna squirmed from his arms, slipped the key in the lock and managed the door. "You seem pretty sure of yourself, fella."

"I am sure." He stared at her for a long moment, his eyes boring into hers.

"I guess that's good."

"It's very good." He winked and followed her into the condo.

She flipped on the lights, then turned. "I've got champagne. Or I can make some coffee."

He took the fingers of her hand and kissed them, featherlight. "There's only one thing I want."

A shiver of anticipation traveled up her spine.

"First, I need to tell you something." His gaze met hers. "I care about you, Adrianna. This isn't playacting for me, not anymore. The only woman I want to date is you."

Their eye contact turned into something more, a tangible connection between the two of them.

Emotion strong and swift rushed over Adrianna. When she looked into his eyes, she saw something that looked a whole lot like love reflected back at her.

Adrianna reached out and touched his cheek, one finger trailing slowly along the rough stubble of his skin until it reached the line of his jaw. "I don't want to date anyone but you either."

"I don't want to kiss anyone but you." His mouth moved up and down her neck, scattering little kisses before his hand slid up to cover her breast. "I don't want to touch anyone but you."

Desire shot through her and her nipple hardened beneath his touch.

"I don't want to make love with anyone but you," she whispered in a husky voice.

His gaze met hers, strong and steady, his blue eyes as dark as the sky before a storm. "You want to make love?"

There was a beat of silence.

"Only," she whispered against his mouth, "with you."

In seconds she found herself pressed against the sofa. They kissed with a feverish intensity that set her blood on fire. Her need for this man was a stark carnal hunger she hadn't even known she was capable of feeling.

Adrianna didn't remember removing her clothes or him removing his, but soon they were naked and he was touching her and caressing her and she was doing the same to him.

She'd been with only one other man in her life and she'd been disappointed. When Tripp's lips moved down her belly and heat enveloped her, Adrianna knew this time would be different.

"Are you protected?" he murmured against her throat.

She stilled. "No," she stammered, "I had no reason—"

"No worries." He closed her lips with his fingers. "I have condoms."

"You carry condoms?"

"Only recently," he said with a chuckle. "I picked up a box when I was in Idaho City."

He grabbed his wallet and pulled out several, keeping one and dropping the rest on the coffee table.

She widened her eyes. "Do you really think we'll need all those?"

"Honey, the way you make me feel, I'm wondering if they'll be enough."

Suddenly, his arms were around her again, and the intense pleasure was back, rolling like large waves propelling her to great heights. His lips were where no man had gone before.

Adrianna told herself to hang on, to make the pleasure last, but the feelings were so strong she couldn't stop it. She clenched the top of his head and bucked up against him, riding the waves until she shuddered.

"I'm sorry," she said.

He lifted his head and brushed the strands of hair back from her face, his eyes still dark.

"Nothing to apologize for," he said in a husky voice that made her blood feel like warm honey sliding through her veins.

"But it's over."

She saw the corner of his mouth twitch as if he was amused by her reaction.

Indignation flooded her. "What's so funny?"

"That was just an appetizer."

"Oh." She felt her cheeks warm.

"I think it's time for the main course," he said with a wink, his erection nudging her leg. "What do you think?"

She planted a kiss at the base of his neck, his skin salty beneath her lips. "I think I'm ready to put in my order."

Tripp slipped out of bed the next morning, careful not to wake Adrianna. He'd kept her pretty busy during the night and wanted to let her sleep.

A smile remained on his lips as he showered, dressed, then started breakfast. By the time Adrianna padded into the kitchen, her hand covering a big yawn, the food and coffee were ready. Her feet were bare and she hadn't bothered dressing, unless you counted an oversize T-shirt. He couldn't be sure, but it appeared she wasn't wearing any underwear beneath the thin white fabric.

His body stirred and for a second he was tempted to forget the food and much-needed caffeine. But he'd seen how little Adrianna ate, so he gestured toward the table. "Sit. I'll serve you."

"You made this?" Her eyes widened at the square white dinner plate filled with a perfectly formed omelet, wheat toast and cut-up pieces of fresh fruit.

"It wasn't easy." Tripp grimaced. "You only had that egg-white mix. No real eggs. No white toast. I couldn't even find regular butter, just that yogurt-blend stuff. When I saw the carton of cream, I thought I was hallucinating."

"I've learned skim milk just doesn't cut it in coffee." Adrianna took a seat, smiling appreciatively when he set a large mug of steaming brew in front of her. He noticed she was wearing the silver heart-shaped pendant he'd given her for her birthday.

"The necklace looks good on you," he said.

"I love it."

They exchanged a smile, then he busied himself fixing a plate for himself and bringing it and the coffee he'd been sipping to the table.

Adrianna took a bite of omelet that he'd spiced up with multi-colored peppers and onion. She looked up and smiled. "This is delicious."

"I'm one of my mother's success stories," Tripp said, attempting to be modest but failing. "Hailey is still a work in progress."

"I'm more like Hailey," Adrianna admitted. "But I want to be more proficient in the kitchen. Did I tell you that your mother offered to give me lessons?"

Tripp froze. He still remembered the big blowup when his mother had offered to show Gayle how to make his favorite potato salad.

"That was so sweet of her," he heard Adrianna say and he released the breath he didn't realize he'd been holding.

His heart, which had stopped beating, jerked back into a normal rhythm. "After breakfast, let's head back to bed."

Adrianna lifted an eyebrow. "I suppose you'd like to spend the day there?"

"What a great idea." He leaned across the table, framed her

face with his hands and kissed her. "I always knew you were a smart woman."

The beautiful brunette's lips twitched. "If you have a full day of activity planned, you'd best eat up, cutie pie, because I'm going to wear you out."

Tripp didn't think that was possible. But, hot damn, what a way to go.

CHAPTER SEVENTEEN

The next week passed quickly. Even though no words of love had been exchanged, Adrianna was convinced Tripp loved her. She could see it in his eyes, feel it in his gentle touch. Sometimes, while they were making love, the words would push against her lips. She held them back, wanting to hear him say them first.

Any day now, she told herself. One of these days he would surprise her by confessing his feelings. Perhaps after tonight's party.

Her lips curved upward as she sat on her bed and bent to tie her shoes. When Mary Karen had first mentioned having a retro-themed party this fall, Adrianna had ordered a poodle skirt and saddle shoes from an online specialty store.

A tingle of anticipation traveled up her spine. This party would be her and Tripp's first big event as a couple since their relationship had undergone a change.

How many years had she dreamed of dating Tripp Randall? Now it was a reality. Being with him was even better than she'd imagined. They talked. They laughed. They made love. Adrianna couldn't remember ever being so happy.

The doorbell rang just as she finished tying the black-and-hot-pink shoelaces around her ponytail. She hurried across the hardwood floors, her heart thumping in her chest.

She opened the door and gasped. While she'd decided to dress in fifties garb, Tripp had chosen the sixties. Adrianna resisted a sudden urge to giggle.

From the leather headband on his head to the huaraches on his feet, Tripp fit the picture of a hippie to perfection.

"I like the fringed vest." She motioned him inside. "And the beads."

He gave her a wink. "Love beads, baby."

"Groovy," she said, giving him a kiss.

"Are you chewing gum?"

"Taste the spearmint?" She snapped the gum, then grinned at his stunned expression.

"Where's my Adrianna?" he teased. "What have you done with her?"

My Adrianna. Oh, how she liked the sound of that.

"She's right here." Adrianna gave in to impulse and twirled in her poodle skirt. "Ready to rock 'n' roll."

"Well, I'm ready to get my groove on." Tripp held out his arm. "Shall we split like a banana?"

Adrianna laughed. Something told her this would be a night to remember.

One of the first people Tripp saw when they walked through the front door of Mary Karen and Travis's large mountain home was his sister, Hailey.

Her mile-high bangs, thick eyeliner and tight designer jeans told him she'd picked the eighties as her decade of choice. Either that or she'd had a serious fashion meltdown.

Tripp tipped his head back and studied her for a moment

longer. The vintage Bon Jovi T-shirt was a nice touch. "Don't you look...interesting."

"Don't mind him." Adrianna stepped forward and gave his sister a quick hug. "You look adorable."

"Thank you." Hailey took a sip from the tall glass of what looked like orange juice but probably wasn't. "So do you."

The outside door opened and a man stepped into the marble foyer resplendent in black leather.

An appreciative look filled Hailey's gaze. "Who's that?"

Tripp exchanged a look with Adrianna. "I'd say, underneath all that leather and swagger is Winn Ferris."

Adrianna narrowed her gaze, then chuckled as the man whipped off his black hat. "You're right. It's Winn."

Hailey took another sip of her drink and stared surreptitiously at Winn through lowered lashes. "He's cute."

"His father is Jim Ferris, who owns the land next to your family's property," Adrianna explained. "Winn is big into golf-course development."

"Is he dating anyone?"

Adrianna shook her head.

"Introduce me," Hailey urged, her blue eyes dancing with interest.

Tripp frowned. Winn had to be at least eight years older than his sister.

He thought about attempting to divert Hailey's attention, but Winn had spotted Adrianna and was headed toward them.

"Adrianna." Winn took her hands and stepped back, his gaze filled with admiration. "You look incredible."

Adrianna flushed. "You look pretty spiffy, yourself. Almost as if you just stepped off the set of *Rebel Without a Cause.*"

"How kind of you to notice." Winn shifted his gaze and acknowledged Tripp with a nod before settling his gaze on Hailey. "Who is this pretty young woman? I don't believe we've met."

The lascivious look in Winn's dark eyes brought Tripp's protective side out in full force.

"This is my *little* sister, Hailey," Tripp said, emphasizing the word before continuing with the introductions.

"Do you live in Jackson Hole, Hailey?" Winn asked. "Or are you just here visiting family?"

Hailey batted her heavily mascaraed lashes at him. "I recently moved back."

"What a coincidence. I just moved here myself." Winn glanced at the drink in her hand. "What's that in your hand?"

Hailey lifted the glass with the orange slice on the rim. "Harvey Wallbanger."

"How about you show me where I can get one of those?"

Hailey flashed him a flirtatious smile. "I'd be delighted."

Tripp stepped forward, but Adrianna grabbed his arm. "I'd like to take a stroll around the house."

"I'd like to tell Winn Ferris to find someone his own age," Tripp growled. "But not you," he hurriedly added.

"She'll be fine." Adrianna stroked his arm in a soothing gesture. "They're surrounded by people. Nothing is going to happen."

Tripp exhaled a breath and forced himself to relax. Adrianna was right. This was a party, not a love-in.

A half hour later, when he and Adrianna were embroiled in a hot game of Twister, he considered retracting that statement. One of his legs was over Adrianna's waist while his head was precariously close to her chest. It was next to impossible to maintain his balance while breathing in the sultry scent of her perfume.

"Sorry," he murmured to her when his face bumped against her breast as David Wahl stretched out his hand in an attempt to reach a yellow circle.

Adrianna giggled and he swore she twisted so that same breast now brushed against his lips.

His mouth went dry. He was face-to-face with her perky nipple, the erect tip clearly visible through her white shirt and lacy bra.

"Ohh." A loud cry went up from the contestants when David's attempt failed and triggered a collapse.

"Let's do it again." July Wahl scrambled out from under the pile of bodies. "I like this game."

Once on his feet, Tripp extended a hand to Adrianna and helped her up. "Do you want to have another go at this or try another game?"

"We need two more participants in the living room," Mary Karen announced from the doorway. "The game is about to begin."

When no one immediately volunteered, the pretty blonde dressed in a short black skirt and white go-go boots with tassels pointed at him and Adrianna. "You two, head to the living room. Stat."

"What game are we playing?" Adrianna asked Mary Karen as they obediently trudged along beside her.

"A fun one," Mary Karen said with a sly smile, glancing at Tripp. "Your good friend Winn Ferris is playing."

"What's the game?" Tripp repeated Adrianna's question as they approached the group sitting on the floor in a circle.

Mary Karen reached down and pulled a bottle from a bag on the floor and held it up. "Spin the bottle, of course."

~

Adrianna took a seat next to Winn, smiled at Hailey and tried not to let her dismay show.

Spin the bottle.

They were adults. Most of those at this party were married. Yet, there was only one man she wanted to kiss this evening and he still stood, arms crossed, as if he had no intention of playing.

"Seriously, Mary Karen. Spin the bottle?" she heard him say.

The lips of the mother of five curved up in an impish smile. "I happen to like kissing."

"She speaks the truth." Her husband, Travis, appeared and snaked an arm around her middle, pulling her close. "Five children are testament to that fact. Give me a kiss, sweetheart."

Mary Karen giggled and planted a kiss on her husband's cheek. "That's all for now."

"Beware of the mistletoe, Mrs. Fisher," Travis teased. "This is your one warning."

Adrianna turned to Lexi, who sat near her. "Mistletoe?"

"Haven't you seen it?" Lexi chuckled. "It's all over the house."

"It's only October," Tripp said mildly, finally sitting down.

"Doesn't matter." Lexi lifted a perfectly manicured hand in an airy wave. "Travis and Mary Karen love mistletoe."

Adrianna shifted her gaze to Tripp. "We'll have to watch out for it."

His eyes darkened. Adrianna smiled. It looked as though she wasn't the only one with kissing on her mind.

"I've never played spin the bottle," Adrianna whispered to him.

"It's the most fun," Tripp said in a low tone, his gaze focused on her bright red mouth, "when the game is rigged."

"Why is that?" she whispered back.

"That way you get to kiss who you want." Tripp leaned close and she knew he'd have planted one on her right then if Travis hadn't pulled him back.

"Whoa—down, boy," the party's host admonished. "Not that I don't applaud such effort, but you have to wait your turn."

"We should have stayed with Twister," Tripp muttered.

Adrianna smiled, but when Mary Karen indicated she should spin the bottle first, she froze, her gaze returning to Tripp.

He lifted his shoulder in a slight shrug and Adrianna reluctantly gave the bottle a hard spin.

She heard Tripp's sharp intake of breath when it landed on Winn *"Rebel Without a Cause"* Ferris.

A broad smile spread across Winn's lips. "It looks as if my luck is on the upswing."

Beside her Tripp muttered a curse and started to rise. She placed a steadying hand on his arm and smiled. With obvious reluctance, he sat back.

Adrianna leaned across the circle and placed a hand on each of Winn's cheeks. Before he could react, she bestowed a big kiss —right in the middle of his forehead.

Laughter filled the circle and Adrianna sat back, triumphant. Tripp grabbed her hand and contentment flowed through her like warm honey.

The way she looked at it, she wouldn't want Tripp kissing another woman, so why would she kiss another man?

When it was Tripp's turn, the bottle landed on his sister, Hailey. The look of mutual revulsion on each of their faces made everyone laugh. He brushed a kiss against her cheek and she made a great show of wiping it off.

Benedict Campbell stepped into the doorway. "What's the game in this room?"

"Sit." Mary Karen leaped up and grabbed his arm, then pointed to an empty spot in the circle. "We're short one man."

Ben looked puzzled but did as she asked. There was something about the petite mother of five's demeanor that made even a pompous orthopedic surgeon obey without question.

Adrianna was trying to figure out what era Ben was supposed to represent in his white suit with bell-bottom pants and wide lapels when she saw the gaudy gold chain around his neck. Late-seventies disco era, she concluded as Hailey leaned forward and gave the bottle a spin.

Around and around it went before coming to a stop on Benedict.

He glanced at Mary Karen.

She smiled. "In case you hadn't figured it out, we're playing spin the bottle. Hailey has to kiss you."

The respected doctor's gaze shifted to Tripp's sister and a look Adrianna couldn't decipher passed between them.

Hailey slanted a sideways glance to see if Winn was watching. The land developer's gaze was firmly fixed on her.

"Well, rules are rules," Hailey said with an exaggerated sigh.

Adrianna expected Ben to protest, but instead, an enigmatic smile crossed his lips.

"You don't have to kiss him," Tripp said, sounding very much like an overprotective older brother.

Hailey responded with a toss of her heavily sprayed hair. "Like I said, I follow the rules."

"Since when?" Tripp scoffed, but Hailey was already wrapping her arms around Ben's neck and gazing into his eyes.

"By the way, I'm Hailey Randall," she murmured. "Nice to meet you."

Instead of kissing him on the cheek as Adrianna expected, Hailey pressed her lips against Ben's slightly parted ones and let her mouth linger an extra heartbeat.

By the time Tripp's sister pulled back, there was a gleam in Ben's eyes and Hailey's cheeks flushed.

"I'm Benedict Campbell." He spoke in a low tone, his gaze never leaving hers. "Because we've already kissed, you can call me Ben."

A titter of laughter erupted from everyone in the circle. Everyone except Tripp and Winn.

Ben's fingers were poised on the bottle when Mary Karen peered into the room and announced the dance party was starting. She instructed everyone to make their way to the back patio for the twist contest.

Instead of immediately heading outside—as Hailey and Ben did—Tripp and Adrianna lingered, chatting with several other couples. Throughout the conversation, Tripp's hand rested lightly against the small of her back.

Happiness bubbled up inside her and Adrianna couldn't keep a smile from her face. Finally, an exasperated Mary Karen returned and marshaled the stragglers toward the back of the house. A bottleneck ensued under a large curved archway when couples kept stopping to kiss.

Adrianna was puzzled until she lifted her gaze. Only then did she spot the small sprig of berries and leaves.

Mistletoe.

Adrianna glanced ahead, looking for Hailey and breathing a sigh of relief when she didn't spot her. She didn't think Tripp could take seeing his "little" sister kiss another man this evening.

Of course, judging by the slender, dark-haired beauty now standing beside Winn Ferris, it appeared he wasn't waiting around for Hailey. Tripp saw the couple the same instant she did. Instead of looking pleased that Winn's focus had shifted from his sister, he scowled.

"I don't recognize his latest companion." Adrianna kept her tone low. "Do you?"

The belt of the woman's mint-colored sixties dress flattered her slender waist while the strand of pearls emphasized the elegant curve of her neck. Her jet-black hair had been teased into a magnificent beehive while thick eyeliner swooped dramatically up at the corners of her eyes.

"She looks familiar," Adrianna mused. "I just can't place her."

"Poppy Westover. She was on the cheer squad."

With Gayle.

Adrianna's mind filled in the words he'd left off. Even though she hadn't thought of Poppy in years, now that Tripp said her name, she recognized her. The woman had been one of Gayle's closest friends in high school. She and Gayle had renewed their friendship when they'd both settled on the East Coast after college.

She'd been at Gayle's funeral. Her hair had been shorter and she'd been wearing glasses.

"Are you going to say hello?" she asked when Tripp remained rooted where he stood.

"No."

Adrianna widened her eyes at his sharp tone.

As if realizing how he sounded, he offered a conciliatory smile. "She's occupied with Winn. It might not even be her."

"It's her." Adrianna sighed.

"I think she's glaring at me," she heard Tripp mutter, but knew she had to have heard wrong.

Anyway, Poppy didn't matter. It was her and Tripp's turn under the mistletoe. Excitement skittered up Adrianna's spine. Tripp would kiss her and everyone would see how much he cared.

Almost of their own accord, her arms rose, ready to wrap around his neck. But he reached out and held them down, pressing a rather perfunctory kiss against her surprised lips.

Before she could even process what had just happened, it was over. He propelled her outside, her elbow cupped in his hand while another couple took their place under the mistletoe.

Confused and seized by a sudden urge to cry, Adrianna blinked rapidly. As her mind raced to make sense of what had just happened, she told herself not to overreact.

Based on how loving Tripp had recently been, his acting as if she didn't mean anything to him made no sense.

Unless...

Adrianna's heart plummeted.

Unless she'd been only kidding herself.

Unless she'd been simply a short-term diversion.

Unless this was Tripp's way of making it clear to everyone that he wasn't interested in anything long-term.

At least not with her.

∼

Tripp felt Poppy's eyes boring into the back of his shirt. Until he'd seen her, he'd been having a stellar evening. Excluding, of course, the moment his baby sister locked lips with Benedict. *That* had been disturbing.

When he'd seen Poppy's stare directed at him, it was as if Gayle herself was standing there, pointing a finger at him, saying, "I knew it. I knew Adrianna was the one you wanted all along. You lied to me, Tripp."

It was, of course, absolutely not true. He'd been totally faithful. He'd loved his wife. Still, just the reminder of Gayle's crazy accusations brought a frigid coldness to his body.

By her silence and surreptitious glances, he could tell Adrianna was puzzled by his change in mood, but he didn't know how to reassure her, how to explain what he was feeling. Not when he didn't fully understand it himself.

When his phone buzzed, Tripp felt as if he'd been granted a reprieve. He pulled it from his pocket and glanced at the readout. "Hi, Mom. What's up?"

"Tripp." His name barely made it past his mother's lips when she began to cry.

Every hair on his body lifted. "What's wrong?"

Beside him, Adrianna went very still.

"Your father, he collapsed." His mom choked out the words. "I called 9-1-1. The rescue squad came. He's on his way to the hospital."

His heart thudded heavily, making him light-headed and nauseous.

"I'm leaving now." Even though Tripp fought to project an aura of calm, he couldn't keep the slight tremor from his voice. "I'll pick you up."

"No, I can drive myself." She took a shuddering breath and then blew her nose. "Just meet me at the hospital."

"I'm leaving now," he assured her, but he spoke into the ether. His mother had already hung up.

Tripp turned to Adrianna, fighting for control. "It's my father."

Worry filled her green eyes. "What's wrong?"

"My dad collapsed. He's on his way to the hospital." Tripp gripped her hand. "I think he's dying."

CHAPTER EIGHTEEN

Even though Tripp received his fair share of curious glances when he, Adrianna and Hailey had shown up in the emergency room in their retro-party garb, the thought of taking time to change never occurred to him.

All that mattered was getting to his father. Quickly.

Shortly after he walked through the doors of the hospital, it became apparent this was far less serious than he'd feared. Thank goodness.

"You take Adrianna and Hailey home." His mother glanced at her now-sleeping husband, his face pale against the pillow. By the time Tripp arrived, his father had already been transferred from the emergency room to a medical-surgical floor for observation. "I'm staying."

"I'll stay with you." Tripp felt as if he'd been given a great gift when the doctor had determined his dad's symptoms were simply a bad reaction to a recent change in medicine. His physician had decided to play it safe and keep him overnight but planned to release him in the morning.

"You go home." His mother's lips lifted in a weary smile. "If you stay, I'll want to visit with you. This way, I can rest between the nurses checking on him."

"You're spending the night?"

She nodded.

"I'll come in the morning, then, and relieve you." Tripp thought quickly, already planning the day. "I can be with him while the doctor makes his rounds. That way you can get some sleep and be rested when he comes home."

"We'll talk about that in the morning," his mother said, making no promises.

Tripp thought about arguing but decided to let it go...for now. Even though his mother needed to rest, getting her to leave her husband of thirty-nine years—even for a few hours—wouldn't be easy.

He took her hand, squeezing it tightly. "Promise you'll call if you need anything."

She assured him she would, but Tripp knew she'd hesitate to disturb him. It didn't matter. He planned to call the nurse's station every couple of hours during the night to check on his dad's status anyway.

He exited the room and saw Hailey and Adrianna approaching with a cup of coffee in each of their hands. They'd offered to go to the snack center at the end of the hall and get coffee for everyone. He knew it had been an excuse to give him some alone time with his mom.

"How's Daddy?" Hailey asked when he drew close, her eyes wide.

"Better." Tripp offered her a reassuring smile, thankful the news was good. "He's sleeping comfortably."

"Good." Hailey expelled a shaky breath, her eyes still red-rimmed from earlier tears.

Tripp shifted his gaze to Adrianna. He'd shamefully neglected her since they'd arrived at the hospital. She'd been a trouper and hadn't complained. "I'm sorry for keeping you out so late. I'll take you home now."

"Your father is your priority. He's a wonderful man. I'm just happy to hear he's doing—" Adrianna broke off as her voice fractured "—better. I can find a ride if you want to stay."

"I appreciate the offer, but Mom kicked me out." Tripp forced a chuckle. "I'll be back in the morning so she can go home and get some rest before he's released."

"I'm staying." Hailey nodded decisively. She held up the cups of steaming coffee in her hands. "This will keep Mom and me going all night and then some."

"It might be best to go home so you're rested when Dad is released. It's your choice," he added when he saw her chin lift in a stubborn tilt.

"I'll talk to Mom. See what she wants."

Tripp rested a hand on her shoulder. "Call me if anything changes."

Tears sprang to Hailey's eyes. "He *is* going to be okay, isn't he?"

For some reason, Tripp found himself glancing at Adrianna.

"He must be doing well if they're talking about releasing him in the morning." Adrianna's tone soothed and reassured not only his sister but Tripp as well. "These kinds of reactions can be scary, but most people bounce back quickly. Your dad is a real fighter."

Hailey fished a tissue from her pocket and wiped away a tear. "Thanks, Adrianna."

A look of puzzlement filled Adrianna's eyes. "What did I do?"

"You're here. You listened to me rattle on and on. You let me cry on your shoulder." Hailey gave a wobbly smile. "I can see why you're so good at your job. You make me believe that everything is going to be okay."

"Well, thank you." Adrianna appeared touched by his sister's declaration. "I *do* believe this is just a minor bump in the road."

Tripp left the hospital via the side entrance. He didn't think he was capable of smiling at one more jokester flashing the peace sign.

He told himself he should keep his distance from Adrianna until he figured things out. But he couldn't stop from reaching for her hand as they headed to the truck. Because, like his sister said, just being with Adrianna made him feel that everything was going to be okay.

~

Instead of taking her to her condo, Tripp surprised Adrianna by asking if she'd spend the night at his place. Even though he'd stayed with her many times, this would be the first time she'd spent the night at his town house.

After what had happened at the party, for an instant the anger and hurt she'd held under tight control reared up and she briefly considered responding with a snarky jab to let him know she was irritated by his behavior under the mistletoe. But he was tired and worried about his father and she'd never been one for such games.

Discussing what had happened at the party could wait for another time.

She accepted his offer but made him stop at her place first to pick up a change in clothes and some needed toiletries for the next morning.

While she wondered what she'd do if he wanted to make love, once they got to his place and crawled into bed, he simply pulled her close and held her tight. Exhausted, they slept the entire night.

Tripp was in a panic the next morning when he realized he hadn't called the hospital once. Before he pulled on his clothes he was on the phone. Adrianna saw the relief on his face after he'd talked with his mother. He'd wanted to go straight to the hospital, but his mother told him they were already signing dismissal papers.

Then his dad had gotten on the phone and insisted they both come out to the ranch for lunch. They could talk more then. Instead of a big breakfast, she and Tripp settled for a quick bowl of cereal.

While she munched on her Shredded Wheat, Adrianna inspected her surroundings. Last night, she'd been too tired—and stressed—to pay much attention.

Tripp had purchased the townhome several months after he'd moved back. His place was less than five miles from Jackson, in a development that was a nice blend of single-family homes and town houses.

"Do you miss living on a ranch?" She cast a wide glance around the professionally decorated living room where everything matched and was in perfect order.

With no personal items or pictures sitting out, the place could have been a show home.

"I don't right now." He came up behind her and kissed the back of her neck. "I'm not here often enough to make it matter. Eventually I'd like to build a place on some of my family's ranchland."

Eventually.

She wondered when that would be. When he married? Had a family?

Adrianna stepped from his embrace and walked to the sink, pouring the remaining milk in her bowl down the drain. "Once I brush my teeth, I'm ready to go."

She glanced down at the jeans and pumpkin-colored T-shirt she'd stuffed into her bag last night and sighed. Even though she wished she were dressed a little better, she knew Kathy wouldn't care.

His mother was a sweetheart. As was his father. Seeing Frank so ill had hit her hard, but Adrianna had done her best not to let her fear show. Without realizing how it had happened, Tripp's parents had become important to her. In fact, she'd come to love them as if they were her own mom and dad.

"I swore it was right here." Tripp shut the cabinet in the living room, a look of dismay on his face.

"I promised Mom I'd bring my extra iPad." His lips lifted in a rueful smile. "Now I can't find it."

"This place is so organized I wouldn't think it'd be hard to locate."

"How about you check around up here?" he said. "I'll look in the basement."

"You sure you want me poking around in your stuff?"

"I don't have anything to hide, Adrianna."

He headed downstairs and she wandered through the main level, trying to think of a logical place he might have stowed it. After rechecking the cabinets in the living room, she moved to the master bedroom.

In the closet, his clothes hung in an orderly fashion. She was pleased to see he had only a handful of shoes and boots. When a man had more shoes than her, it always made her suspicious.

Nothing jumped out from the shelf above the clothing racks except a large brown box. As organized as Tripp was, she could imagine him placing his rarely used small electronics all in one place.

The box was surprisingly heavy. She placed it on the closet floor, then tugged it out into the main part of the bedroom before looking inside. The scattered pictures on top told her this wasn't a box of electronics. This was Gayle's stuff.

She recognized the ultrasound picture Gayle had emailed her. There were baby-shower cards intermixed with pictures of her and Tripp. Pictures of a very pregnant Gayle looking radiant stared back at her. She lifted a pregnancy journal and flipped through it, noticing that it was almost complete.

"What are you doing?" Tripp's voice sliced the air like a whip.

Adrianna stiffened, dropping the journal back into the box. "I thought this might have electronics in it."

His expression was closed, guarded. "I'm sure you didn't need to bring it out of the closet to realize you were incorrect."

He's stressed about his dad, she told herself and bit back a harsh reply.

"When was the last time you looked through this stuff?" she asked instead.

Tripp didn't answer. He simply lifted the box back on the top shelf.

"Gayle looked so happy in those pictures," Adrianna said cautiously.

He held out his hand to her. "We'll be late."

Adrianna let him draw her from the bedroom, casting one last glance in the direction of the closet. Why wouldn't Tripp discuss Gayle with her?

For that matter, why had he given her such a chaste kiss under the mistletoe?

She thought she'd gotten to know Tripp pretty well this past month. Now she had to wonder if she knew him at all.

Lunch with his parents was a pleasant affair. Frank was in high spirits. It was hard for Adrianna to believe the man who joked and laughed over chicken and dumplings was the same one who'd been rushed to the hospital less than twenty-four hours ago in an ambulance.

To allow Kathy to relax with her husband, Adrianna and Hailey offered to clean up. Tripp insisted on helping. She watched him filling the dishwasher and a surge of love swamped her.

"Your mom makes the best dumplings," Adrianna said as she

wiped the counter. "I hope she doesn't feel like she always has to cook a big meal when I come out."

Tripp looked up and smiled. "She enjoys cooking. And she likes spoiling you."

Spoiling, Adrianna thought with a warm flush of pleasure, was something a mother would do.

"Well, I always love whatever she makes." Adrianna patted her lean hips. "Though I think I've gained weight from all her good foods."

"You're perfect the way you are." Tripp straightened and pulled her to him, turning strands of her hair loosely around his fingers. "Absolutely, positively perfect."

He kissed her then, long dreamy kisses that sent warmth flowing through her veins like honey.

With a contented sigh, Adrianna wrapped her arms around his broad shoulders. Her head fit perfectly against his chest, just under his chin. Now, this was more like it. "Compliments like that are going to get you every—"

"Break it up, you two." Hailey entered the kitchen, her hands filled with dessert cups with the remnants of strawberry shortcake.

Adrianna started at the interruption. She tried to put some distance between her and Tripp but didn't get far. He kept one arm around her waist.

Once Hailey had placed the dishes on the counter, she turned to her brother. "I can't figure you out, Tripp Randall."

Tripp grinned and played with a lock of Adrianna's hair. "Thanks for the compliment. I like being a mysterious kind of guy."

A chuckle formed low in Adrianna's throat. She opened her mouth to tell Hailey not to encourage him when his sister continued.

"This thing with you and Adrianna," Hailey mused, her brow furrowed. "It's confusing. Not just to me."

Adrianna's breath froze.

Tripp dropped his hand from Adrianna's waist and tilted his head back, his gaze firmly fixed on his sister. "What are you babbling about?"

"At the retro party." Hailey rested against the counter. "You know, I had people actually ask me if you two were dating or just friends."

"Who asked you that?" he asked, clearly puzzled. "And why?"

"While I didn't see it myself—" Hailey paused "—the consensus seemed to be that when it was your turn under the mistletoe, you kissed Adrianna like she was a good buddy."

A wave of humiliation washed over Adrianna. It was bad enough *she'd* noticed it. Her cheeks burned, knowing everyone had been talking about her and Tripp.

Tripp's brows slammed together.

"*If* I kiss Adrianna, *the way* I kiss Adrianna is none of your business," he snapped. "It's no one else's business either. Besides, Adrianna happens to like the way I kiss her. Isn't that right, sweetheart?"

"Well, actually—" Adrianna began.

"Okay, okay." Hailey rolled her eyes. "I was just curious. By the way, Dad said to remind you Radley Meints is coming over Thursday, so make sure the meeting is on your calendar."

"I'll be there," Tripp said.

Adrianna cleared her throat, her insides still churning over that "good buddy" comment. "Who's Radley Meints?"

"He's a political adviser." Tripp straightened and wiped his hands on a dish towel. "We're going to discuss what's involved in mounting a campaign for mayor."

"You're seriously considering running?"

A watchful look filled his eyes. "Sounds like you don't approve."

"It's not up to me to approve or not," she said lightly, turning away. "I just didn't know your plans were this far along."

Had Tripp ever mentioned meeting with a political adviser? No, he hadn't. That was something she'd have remembered. A twinge of disappointment mixed with rising anger nipped at her.

"I need to know what you think, Adrianna," he said. "This will affect you, too."

She forced a little laugh. "How will it affect me?"

"You know how politics is...anyone close to me will be under the microscope."

Close to him. That was her. His good buddy.

"It's your life, Tripp. You have to do what's right for you," she said in a noncommittal "buddylike" tone. "Once we've cleaned this up, I think you'd better take me home. Tomorrow is going to be a busy day."

CHAPTER NINETEEN

Tripp was thankful when Monday morning dawned and he could go into the office. Ever since Saturday night, he'd felt off-balance. He'd been happy that his dad had been able to return home Sunday, but the relaxing day he'd anticipated hadn't materialized.

First Adrianna had found the box. He couldn't blame her for getting into his closet because he'd given her carte blanche to search his home. But standing in the doorway, seeing her looking through Gayle's things had been...difficult.

It was like watching his past and present collide. Like seeing Poppy, the box of photos and baby stuff had brought back memories—and emotions—he thought he'd put to bed. Or at least had under better control.

He tried to concentrate on his computer monitor, but instead of the spreadsheet of figures, he saw Gayle's smiling face on their last day together just before she'd left for the cabin in the mountains. He'd kissed her goodbye, promising to join her as soon as his late-afternoon meeting was over.

Even though Gayle had experienced some ambivalence about the pregnancy early on, she'd seemed excited and happy that day.

When he'd gotten the phone call telling him both his wife and baby had died, Tripp's mind had gone blank. It was as if he'd heard the words but couldn't comprehend. They were both...gone. No warning. No time to say goodbye.

He remembered swallowing against rising nausea. Once his brain had started buzzing, the pain had hit like a Mack truck.

Everyone had told Tripp to give it time, assured him that the pain would lessen. They were right. No one had warned there would be all those dark days first, when he wished he'd died with them.

Adrianna's texts had been a bright spot during that hard period. He realized he'd never thanked her. Never told her how much those friendly contacts had meant to him.

A buzz sounded and he automatically pushed the intercom button, welcoming the reprieve from his thoughts. "Yes?"

"A Ms. Poppy Westover to see you, sir," Paula said in her official voice. "She's not on your schedule. I wasn't sure of your availability—"

"I've got time." Tripp pushed back his chair and rose to his feet. "Please send her in."

Seconds later, Poppy strolled into his office. Gone were the beehive and exaggerated makeup, the pearls and the sixties dress. In their places were sleek dark hair, trendy amber glasses and a dress with blocks of colors that reminded him of fall.

She looked, he thought, more New York City than Jackson Hole.

He rounded the desk to greet her.

"Poppy—" he extended both hands "—I'm glad you stopped by. We didn't get a chance to visit on Saturday."

"Thanks for seeing me." Her red lips curved up in a smile and she gave his fingers a brief squeeze.

"I like the glasses." He gestured for her to take a seat, then took the one beside her. "Are they new?"

"Relatively recent," she admitted. "Wearing contacts had

become a chore. But I desperately need the vision correction. Without glasses, I can barely see ten feet."

She'd been squinting at the party, he realized, not scowling. Some of the tension he'd held inside eased. They hadn't had a chance to talk privately after Gayle's death. At the funeral, he'd gotten the feeling she blamed him for letting Gayle go to the cabin alone.

"I probably should have phoned for an appointment." She sounded uncharacteristically unsure. "I hope I'm not interrupting any lunch plans."

Tripp glanced at the clock on the wall. He hadn't even realized it was already that time. He briefly wondered if Adrianna was available, then remembered she'd told him her day would be a busy one.

"I haven't eaten. If you don't have plans we could grab a bite. Catch up." Tripp may have spoken impulsively, but inviting her felt right. She'd been a good friend to Gayle and to him.

A look of surprise followed quickly by pleasure crossed Poppy's face. "I'd like that."

"Are you in the mood for anything in particular?"

She gave a little laugh. "Is Perfect Pizza still in operation?"

He nodded.

"When I first moved to New York, I craved their chicken Tuscany."

"The pizza with the cream-cheese topping."

A touch of pink colored her cheeks. "I know it's rather decadent, but hey, you only live once."

True, he thought, *and sometimes not for all that long.* Tripp pulled his thoughts back to the woman beside him. "Will Bill be able to join us? It'd be great to see him again."

Okay, that might be stretching the truth a bit. Poppy's husband, Bill Stanhope, was a prominent NYC neurosurgeon. He'd been divorced with grown kids when he and Poppy had met and married. Bill was arrogant and a bit of a jerk, but for old times' sake, Tripp could endure his company for an hour or two.

"Bill is ancient history." Poppy lifted a hand in an airy wave, but for a brief second he saw a hint of sadness in her eyes. "We separated a couple years ago. Our divorce was final last January."

"I'm sorry to hear that." Tripp *was* sorry. Even though he hadn't cared for the guy, Poppy had once seemed very happy with Stanhope.

"Yes, well." She glanced at the Apple watch on her slender wrist. "I need to run a quick errand. Would meeting there at 12:45 work for you?"

He smiled. "I'll see you then."

Once Poppy left, Tripp refocused on the screen, trying to get a few more minutes of work done, but again he found it difficult to concentrate.

He thought about texting Adrianna to see how her day was going, but held back. Tripp wondered if this growing need for her, if this involvement with her, was a mistake. They'd gone so quickly from friends to casual lovers to his wanting to be with her all the time. Which was a problem. He wasn't ready for a full-fledged relationship. He didn't have the time. Like now—here he was thinking of her when he should be working.

If he did commit to running for mayor, his days and nights would be packed to the brim with meetings, fundraisers and required events.

But what was the solution? Walk away from Adrianna? The sick feeling in the pit of his belly told him he may have already waited too long for that to be an option.

No, he told himself. No promises had been made. No words of love exchanged.

The tension gripping his chest eased. When he looked at the screen, the spreadsheet beckoned.

With one eye on the clock, he resumed working.

~

Adrianna's Monday started off far earlier than she'd anticipated. One of the patients who'd been scheduled for an induction that morning had shown up at the hospital with food poisoning at 4:00 a.m.

Even though Adrianna had gone to bed early, racing thoughts had kept sleep at bay. Still groggy, Adrianna had jumped out of bed and headed to the hospital. Dr. Michelle Davis, one of the ob-gyns she worked with, had beaten her there. Her colleague had taken one look at Adrianna's pale complexion and red eyes and teasingly asked if she was certain she hadn't had any of the macaroni salad the patient had ingested.

Adrianna had responded that not everyone looked as good as Michelle did without makeup, then squirted a stream of Visine into her eyes.

While Michelle tended to the food-poisoning patient, Adrianna had turned her attention to a forty-two-year-old first-time mother who was past her due date and also scheduled for an induction. Preferring to go the natural route, the pregnant woman had been given a tincture of black and blue cohosh.

The herbs had worked remarkably well and labor had progressed rapidly. Even as the new mom and her husband were cuddling their baby girl, Karla Anderson had shown up at the emergency room, distraught and crying.

Karla advised the E.R. doc that the last time she'd felt her baby move had been over twenty-four hours earlier. Dr. Wahl, one of the doctors on duty, had been unable to pick up a heartbeat. Concerned, he'd contacted Adrianna, and Karla had been transferred to the maternity area.

There was a quality of unreality to the situation, Adrianna had thought. Karla had been in only last week for her monthly ante-partum visit and the pregnancy had been progressing normally. Yet, the additional tests confirmed the E.R. doc's findings.

Adrianna sat down with Karla, held the young woman's trembling hands and explained her baby would be stillborn. Adrianna was surprised at how calm and rational she sounded when her heart was breaking inside. She cradled the sobbing Karla in her arms and held her for the longest time.

Once hospital social worker Lexi Delacourt arrived, they quietly and gently informed Karla of her options. After more tears, Karla chose to wait until her mother got back into town at the end of the week instead of being immediately induced. She was on the phone with the baby's father when Adrianna slipped from the room, leaving the young woman in Lexi's capable hands.

It was barely one o'clock and Adrianna felt like an old dish towel hung out to dry, whipping in a brisk breeze. She needed Tripp. Needed to feel his arms around her. Needed his comfort. His warmth.

It isn't weakness, she told herself. When you love someone, you're there for them. And they're there for you.

She hadn't heard from him, but then, she'd told him she'd be tied up most of the day and he'd mentioned something about finishing up a big presentation. Adrianna knew how single-minded Tripp could be once he got involved in a project. If she was lucky, he'd be in his office. If she was even luckier, he'd be alone.

Adrianna changed out of her scrubs and freshened up before heading to the executive office suites. Paula was at her desk. The personal assistant gave her a quizzical look when she saw her. She wondered if it was the lack of makeup or the dark circles under her eyes.

"I'm here to see Tripp."

"He left for lunch a little while ago." Paula looked confused. "I thought he was meeting you."

Adrianna fought to keep the disappointment from her voice. "He probably had a business meeting."

"I don't think so." Paula's brows puckered. "He mentioned something about chicken Tuscany at Perfect Pizza. That's not a place he'd typically choose for a business meeting."

Adrianna paused. Would he have gone out to lunch alone? Yes, especially if he was in the mood for that kind of pizza. Her hopes rose.

"Shall I have him call you?" Paula offered. "Tell him you stopped by?"

"No need." Adrianna waved a vague hand. "I'll catch up with him later."

When she left Tripp's office, Adrianna headed out the front door of the hospital. It was a glorious fall day with a crisp bite to the air, but Adrianna barely noticed. Normally she loved hearing the crackle of dried leaves crunching beneath her feet. Today, they were an irritation, scattering dust across the tops of her shoes.

The plan had been to simply walk for several blocks, stretch her legs, then return to the clinic for her late-afternoon appointments. Or so she told herself. Before she knew it, she was downtown. Because Perfect Pizza was just off the main square, she decided to take a quick detour and see if Tripp was still there. See if he wanted company.

She stepped inside the café and smiled at the young man behind the counter waiting to take her order.

"I'm meeting someone," she informed him before turning toward the dining room with its knotty pine booths and picnic-style log tables.

She spotted Tripp immediately. Her heart, which had lurched in her chest at the sight of him, suddenly dropped to her toes. He wasn't alone.

Poppy Westover sat across the table from him, her dark hair shimmering in the overhead fluorescent lights. They were laughing, Adrianna noted dispassionately. While she watched, Poppy reached over and playfully took his hand.

It was the maraschino cherry on the top of a rotten morning. Adrianna edged back from the dining area, not wanting to be seen. Wishing she hadn't seen...

"Did you find your friend?" the boy behind the counter asked.

"He must have already left." Before he could ask any more questions, Adrianna was out the door. The breeze was cool against her hot cheeks as she turned toward the clinic.

Tripp noticed Adrianna was unusually quiet over dinner at The Coffeepot. It wasn't as if she'd been busy eating. She'd barely touched the catfish on her plate. He filled the silence, talking about everything from his father's recent lab work to his upcoming board of trustees presentation.

Even though Adrianna smiled in all the right places and made sounds of acknowledgment, something in her eyes, in the rigid set of her shoulders, worried him.

"I stopped by to see if you were free for lunch today." She waited to speak until the waitress had refilled their iced tea and left the check on the table.

"I'm sorry I missed you," he said, encouraged by the fact she was ready to converse.

When he'd first told her about his day, he hadn't mentioned seeing Poppy because it didn't seem all that relevant. Perhaps he'd been wrong to omit it. "Poppy stopped by. We had lunch at Perfect Pizza."

Adrianna offered a brittle smile.

"I found out she was squinting at the party—" he forced a laugh "—not glaring at me. She needs her glasses to see but didn't wear them because they were too modern for her outfit."

Something flickered in Adrianna's cool green eyes when he paused to take a breath.

Tripp pressed his lips together to stop the rambling.

"Hmm."

"What do you mean by 'hmm'?" he asked, feeling guilty but not knowing why. Feeling frustrated, too.

She traced a finger on the tabletop. "I've been doing a lot of thinking lately."

"About what?"

She straightened in her chair. "Our relationship."

A quick chill sprinted up his spine and he noticed the coolness in her eyes had leeched into her voice.

"What about our relationship?" He found himself stumbling over the words.

"You're a busy man, Tripp. You don't have time to date."

It had been what he'd told himself all along. Why, then, did it sound wrong coming from her lips?

He pulled his brows together. "Is this because I had lunch with Poppy and forgot to tell you?"

"You didn't *forget*," she snapped, then ran her fingers through her hair. She blew out a breath. When she spoke again her voice was calm and well-modulated. "Anyway, I'm not your keeper."

"That's right. You're not." At his raised voice, several patrons at nearby tables turned to stare. When he spoke again, his voice was conciliatory. "Look, I'm sorry. I should have told you about the lunch. We did a lot of reminiscing about Gayle, that's all."

"Oh." A look Tripp couldn't decipher crossed her face. "You can talk to her about Gayle, but not to me?"

Tripp held on to his temper with both hands. It was almost as if Adrianna was spoiling for a fight. Well, he wasn't going to give her one.

"If you have something to say, just say it," he said in as mild a tone as he could muster.

"The box of Gayle's stuff," she reminded him. "I tried to talk to you about her then, but you shut me down. She was my friend, too."

She was also jealous of you.

For a second he thought he'd spoken the words aloud. Words he'd vowed never to say to her. Adrianna didn't deserve to have the memory of her friendship with Gayle tarnished by unjustified accusations spoken in the heat of anger.

After speaking with Poppy today, Tripp felt he understood a little better what had driven Gayle. Poppy firmly believed his wife's insecurities had stemmed from her father's infidelities. His cheating had affected Gayle much more than Tripp realized.

The fact that Gayle had feared Adrianna would be a better match for him had further fueled her insecurities.

Although Tripp had loved Gayle deeply, he reluctantly admitted—but only to himself—that he and Adrianna *were* a better match. Adrianna enjoyed spending time with him and his family. She loved Jackson Hole and while her job was important to her, it wasn't her life.

It amazed him that once he'd opened that door, Adrianna had so quickly become an integral part of his life.

Yet, the depth of his feelings had terrified him. Losing Gayle had thrown him into a black hole that had taken him down so low that he'd wondered many times if he'd survive. What if something happened to Adrianna? Could he put himself in a position of caring so much again?

"It's just not working between us."

Whoa. Hold the damn horses. He pulled his thoughts back to the conversation, to the woman sitting across from him, her face an expressionless mask. "What did you say?"

"This thing between us is not working. It's best we end it now."

Fear, stark and unwelcome, wrapped itself around Tripp's throat, making breathing difficult. "Tell me exactly what's not working."

She lifted that blasted shoulder in another shrug.

In that moment she reminded him of Gayle. All those times she'd refused to share feelings and concerns with him.

Still, as much as a tiny voice inside told him this might be for the best, he couldn't lose Adrianna. He tried again.

"I believe openness and honesty are essential for any relationship to succeed." Considering that his insides quivered like gelatin, he did a good job keeping his voice calm.

She gave a humorless chuckle. "Really?"

"Really." His gaze never left hers.

"It surprises me that you'd say that considering you never told me about your conversation with Poppy."

"I did tell you—"

"Or of your decision to fully explore a mayoral bid. Then there's the matter of your refusal to discuss Gayle with me. And let's not forget that lukewarm kiss under the mistletoe Saturday night. What was going on there, Tripp? Because you're all about being open and honest—why don't you be all open and honest and tell me what was going on in your head at that moment?"

He thought back to Saturday night, to the strong feelings for Adrianna welling up inside him, to the shock of seeing Poppy and being reminded of Gayle's tirades. All he knew was, when he'd stepped under the mistletoe, he'd been seized with an intense need to step back, to regroup.

"I'm not sure what happened at the party," he said, hoping she'd hear the sincerity in his tone. "I'm still trying to sort it out."

"Well, I figured it out, so let me explain it for you." Bright swaths of color crossed Adrianna's high cheekbones. "You like me. Just not enough. You want to let me down easy, but because you're not sure how to do it, you're pushing me away, hoping I'll be the one to walk."

Tripp paused. Pushing her away? If he was, it had been on a subconscious level.

She picked up on his hesitation, and something that looked

like sadness crossed her face. It was gone so quickly he thought he'd just imagined it.

"It was good while it lasted, Tripp. But I need more. I deserve more." She pushed back her chair and stood.

Then, with her back ramrod straight, Adrianna walked out the door and out of his life.

CHAPTER TWENTY

By the next day all of her friends knew she and Tripp were no longer seeing each other. For once Adrianna didn't mind the gossip mill of a small community. It saved her from having to break the news.

Still, her day was filled with well-meaning questions and concerned glances. She planned to go home, grab a dinner from the freezer and lose herself in a good book. Then she received a better offer.

The call from Betsy came midafternoon. Ryan had a meeting that night and she asked if Adrianna was interested in a pizza party and movie. It would be just the two of them—four if you counted Nathan and Puffy.

Even though Adrianna had no doubt Betsy would try to pry out of her the reason for the breakup, the alternative was to sit home and cry over a frozen dinner of rubbery chicken.

Grabbing the pizza box, Adrianna sauntered up to the small cottage. Tonight she and her oldest and dearest friend would enjoy food, conversation and a movie with a happy ending. Adrianna could trust Betsy not to bring up the subject of Tripp. At least not until Adrianna had some pizza in her.

Her friend met her at the door, the baby nestled in her arm.

"I'm so glad you were available." Betsy's warm smile was like a balm to Adrianna's aching heart. "It feels like forever since we've had a girls' night."

Adrianna smiled and stepped inside onto the shiny hardwood floor. A faint scent of vanilla hung in the air.

Puffy trotted out to greet her, looked her up and down, then pranced away.

"How's Puffy?" Adrianna asked. "Is she jealous of the baby?"

"Not at all." Betsy gestured for Adrianna to put the pizza box on the coffee table in the living room next to the plates, napkins and forks that were already there.

Once she did, Betsy handed her son to Adrianna. "I'll get the drinks. Do you want tea? Or I have beer if you're in the mood for something a little stronger."

Adrianna thought about asking her friend if she had any Coyote Gold margarita mix, but decided against it. Alcohol never went well with the blues.

"Tea will be fine." Adrianna inhaled the fresh baby scent from the child in her arms. She dropped her gaze and found serious eyes staring up at her.

"How are you, Nathan?" She took his little hand in her fingers and moved it up and down. "You're a handsome boy. Yes, you are."

If she and Tripp had a child, he might look like this one with dark hair from her and blue eyes from him. Or the baby could get her green eyes and his blond hair. Or—

Stop. Adrianna screwed her eyes shut against the pain. There would be no babies for her and Tripp. Her relationship with him was over. Done. Finished.

"Where did Ryan go tonight?" she asked Betsy when her friend returned, eager to refocus her thoughts.

"He's meeting with some of the guys about Keenan's appeal."

Some of the guys. Tripp?

Adrianna blinked away the image of tousled blond hair and blue eyes. "Do you think your brother will get a new trial?"

"The petition has been filed." Betsy placed the heavy tumblers filled with ice and tea on the coasters on the coffee table before taking a seat on the sofa. "I want it to happen so badly I can taste it. But, like I've said before, I'm trying not to get my hopes up. That's why I decided to stay home tonight. If it all falls through, I'll be devastated."

Adrianna sighed. "I know the feeling."

"What happened with you and Tripp, Adrianna?" Betsy appeared genuinely puzzled. "Did he get scared? Is that why he called it off?"

Adrianna stiffened. This was the part of the gossip that infuriated her. The assumption that Tripp had been the one to call things off. "I broke up with him."

"You're kidding." The shock on Betsy's face would have been laughable at any other time.

Adrianna felt oddly disappointed.

"You've loved him since you were a teenager," Betsy continued, and Adrianna realized that having a friendship that went way back wasn't always a good thing.

She took a sip of tea, carefully schooling her features. "I'm not the one for him."

"Is this about Gayle?" Not bothering with plates or forks, Betsy lifted a slice of pizza from the box and took a bite. "After seeing the two of you together...I really thought he was over her."

Before Adrianna could speak, Puffy strutted back into the room and hopped onto a nearby chair.

Adrianna shifted uncomfortably beneath the Pomeranian's unyielding stare. In her arms, Nathan began to stir.

Betsy dropped her slice onto a plate and reached for her baby. "I'll put him in his Pack 'n Play. That way we can keep an eye on him."

Giving up the warm bundle snuggled against her chest was

hard, but Adrianna handed the baby to her friend, hoping this interruption would be a perfect opportunity to change the subject. Once Betsy resumed sitting, Adrianna smiled. "How do you like yours?"

"I love my Pack 'n Play." Betsy reached over and took her hand. "Do you really want to talk about baby equipment?"

"More than I want to talk about Tripp," she quipped.

A look of compassion settled over Betsy's face. "Tell me what happened."

"I don't want to talk about it." To her horror, tears welled in her eyes. "Or him."

She blinked rapidly at Betsy and Puffy. Both had pity in their eyes. "He was mounting a campaign for mayor and didn't even tell me."

"He never mentioned it?"

"Well, maybe once," Adrianna grudgingly admitted, "in passing."

Betsy thoughtfully chewed on a bite of pizza. "Is that why you broke up with him? Because he withheld that fact?"

There was no condemnation in her tone, only curiosity.

"That's right." Adrianna lifted the glass of tea to her mouth with shaky hands.

Puffy barked once, her dark eyes firmly fixed on Adrianna.

Puzzled, Adrianna glanced at Betsy. "What does she want?"

"She doesn't believe that's the whole story," Betsy said with an airy wave. "Neither do I."

Adrianna shifted uncomfortably. "Okay, so maybe the reason is a little more complicated."

She found herself slanting a glance at Puffy, who remained silent. The dog's deep brown eyes bored into her, demanding she further explain. "I have all these jumbled-up feelings I can't decipher."

"I think I know you pretty well." Betsy's voice was solemn, her eyes serious. "Do you mind if I take a whack at it?"

"Yes, I mind," Adrianna retorted.

Betsy grinned. "Well, I'm going to give you my theory anyway."

Adrianna settled back against the sofa and crossed her arms. "If you feel you must," she said stiffly.

"When you were growing up, you focused your romantic fantasies on Tripp, not only because he was good-looking and kind, but unattainable."

Confused, Adrianna cocked her head.

"It's the same reason teenagers fall in love with rock stars and actors. They're safe. You know you're free to fantasize and love them from afar."

"I never stopped liking Tripp."

Puffy gave a staccato bark.

Adrianna whirled toward the dog. "It's true."

"Think carefully," Betsy urged.

"He was at another school," Adrianna protested. "And in love with Gayle. Then, married."

"You didn't answer my question."

"I didn't think of him in the same way then."

Puffy stared for a second, then bent to lick a paw.

"What about after that jerk you were dating disappointed you?"

"I may have thought about him a time or two after that," Adrianna admitted.

"You refocused on Tripp because you were scared. You didn't want to give your heart to someone new because you might be hurt. Tripp was safe. He was married. Even after he lost his wife, he was on the East Coast, two thousand miles away."

Adrianna pondered the words and swore she saw Puffy nod.

"What does that have to do with now?" Adrianna asked. "I've gotten to know Tripp well since he moved back, even better once we began dating."

"I'm thinking that once you got to know him, the blinders

were off. You didn't like what you saw." Betsy's tone was matter-of-fact. "That's natural. We build someone up in our mind and often once we really get to know them, we discover they aren't that great of a person."

"Tripp Randall is a wonderful man," Adrianna said indignantly, sitting bolt-upright. "He's caring. He's compassionate. I won't allow you to speak badly of him."

Betsy lifted a glass of tea to her lips, partially hiding a smile. "If he's so wonderful, why break up with him?"

The decision to call it quits with Tripp had been an impulsive one, brought on by a stressful day. But the underlying reasons that had troubled her, that had fueled that decision, remained. "While I think Tripp cares about me, perhaps even loves me, I'm not his soul mate."

Adrianna stumbled over the word, remembering the conversation she'd overheard between Tripp and Hailey. "I know you think what I felt for Tripp when I was young was simply infatuation. There was this moment, when I was fourteen, and our eyes locked…"

Her heart fluttered, remembering the connection. "I looked into his eyes and, for me, something clicked." Adrianna gave a little laugh. "It was probably just an overactive adolescent imagination."

Betsy—and Puffy—remained silent.

"I could lie and tell myself that even if he didn't love me quite as much, I loved him enough for both of us. But I can't do it. I want to be first in my husband's heart. I want him to kiss me senseless—anytime, anywhere—simply because he's crazy about me. I don't think that's asking for too much." By the time she finished, Adrianna was breathing hard, as if she'd just run a long race.

A race she'd lost. A race that was over before it had begun.

Puffy jumped off the chair and hopped up on the sofa. The

Pomeranian rested her head on Adrianna's lap and expelled a heavy sigh.

"My sentiments exactly, Puffball." Adrianna stroked the dog's soft hair and let a wave of sadness wash over her. "Sometimes life sucks."

~

I need more. I deserve more.

The last words Adrianna had said to him played over and over in Tripp's mind, like one of those records his father spun on his old-fashioned turntable. Tripp's business mind had mentally noted all the complaints she'd lodged. He didn't talk to her about Gayle, hadn't immediately told her about meeting Poppy for lunch or mentioned he was conferring with someone about mounting a campaign for mayor.

His anger rose. What if he didn't want to discuss Gayle with her? Most women would be happy not to have a man bring up a former woman in his life. And he *had* told her about Poppy and about looking into running for mayor.

Tripp raked his fingers through his hair. Why hadn't she just told him the truth? She'd wanted out. Adrianna just plain didn't want him anymore.

The thought was a lightning bolt to his heart, the pain hot and searing. Strong enough to bring moisture to his eyes, which he quickly wiped away.

It was for the best, he told himself. If losing her now hurt this much—and he was man enough to admit that it *did* hurt—how much worse would it have been in a year? Ten?

The doorbell rang and Tripp bit back an expletive. All morning the buzzer had sounded with kids selling candy, popcorn and cookies. Today was only the beginning. They'd be coming all week. Until now he'd bought from every one of them. He didn't need any more candy, cookies or interruptions.

He strode across his living room and jerked open the door. "Look, I already bought—"

"Good morning to you, too." His mother slipped past him and stood poised by the living room sofa. "Can I stay if I promise not to try to sell you anything?"

Tripp grabbed pieces of newspaper off the floor and kicked a pair of shoes behind a chair. Since Adrianna had walked out of his life, he'd found it difficult to summon much energy for household chores. "Is Dad okay?"

"He's fine. Sends his love. I'm here because you haven't returned my calls. Your office said you were working from home." Her brows furrowed in motherly worry. "You look terrible."

"I'm okay." Every day was easier, he told himself, though he recognized the lie. "Great, in fact."

She settled herself on the sofa. "I heard you and Adrianna aren't together anymore."

He braced himself, ready for her to expound on how perfect they were for each other and what a fool he was for letting her go. God knew he'd heard that little sermon enough the past couple of days. That was one of the reasons he'd decided to work from home today. He couldn't stand the sympathetic looks and the advice.

"I'm sorry," his mother said.

He widened his eyes in surprise.

"I know you're hurting, son," she said softly. "Is there anything I can do?"

His laugh was devoid of humor. "I thought you'd be telling me that I need to go to her, to make amends for whatever it was I'd done. Telling me you love her and she's the best thing that ever happened to me."

"There's no need for me to say it." His mother leaned forward. "You know all those things. For whatever reason, that's not the path you've chosen to take."

Tripp dropped down into a chair to face her. He blew out a breath. "It's not that I don't want to make amends. I just think that perhaps it's better this way."

"Do you love her?" The question was so soft and low that for a second he wondered if he'd only imagined it.

"I do," he said, then decided to bare his soul. "I believe I love her more than I did Gayle. Does that shock you?"

His mother's gaze searched his. "Why should that shock me?"

"Because Gayle and I were together forever." He paused and took a deep breath. "Yet, things were often hard between us. With Adrianna, everything seems easy."

"To be fair, there will be difficult times with Adrianna. Anytime you're with someone a long time, there are valleys as well as peaks. That said, I do believe you and Adrianna are a better match."

"That's what Gayle thought." He gave a harsh chuckle. "I can't count the number of times she told me to leave, to go to Adrianna."

His mother's eyes widened. "You and Adrianna were involved while you were married?"

"No. No, of course not." Tripp closed his eyes for a second and gathered his composure. "Can I get you something to drink? I don't have much, but—"

"Why would Gayle say such things to you?"

"She was jealous. Way back when we were in high school, she told me she didn't think Adrianna was pretty. I disagreed. She got upset and we had a big fight. It was around the time her parents split."

"When her mother found out her father had been cheating on her for years," his mother mused.

"I put it off to that, but it got so every time we argued she'd bring up Adrianna. Then she started saying Adrianna would be better for me. It hurt." Tripp leaned forward and met his mother's gaze. "I loved my wife. I was faithful to her, body, mind and soul."

"I know, son." His mother reached over and squeezed his hand. "In her heart, Gayle knew that, too."

They sat in silence for several heartbeats.

"Losing her and the baby..." Tripp visibly shuddered. "I never want to go through that again."

His mother's eyes were solemn. "It hurts to lose someone you love."

"I can't go through that again," Tripp repeated. "I *won't* go through that again."

"I'm afraid you don't get that option," his mother said softly. "None of us do. Death is a part of life."

Tripp lifted his chin. "I won't put myself in that position."

His mother tilted her head. "You love me and your father."

"Of course."

"And Hailey."

"Yes." He pulled his brows together. "But what—"

"Something could happen to any of us at any time," she said quietly. "You're already in the position you're determined to avoid."

"My feelings for Adrianna are so strong already that—" He stopped. "I can't imagine how much stronger they'll be in five, twenty or even forty years."

His mother placed a hand on his arm, stopping his words. "It isn't the loss you should fear, but never loving. Finding that someone is rare. It's a very special gift, one not to be tossed aside lightly."

Silence sat between them for several seconds.

"If I lose Frank—" his mother paused and cleared her throat "—I'll take the pain and be thankful for all the wonderful years he and I've shared."

Tripp leaned back in his chair and dug his thumbs against his nose. "I blew it."

"Probably."

He jerked his head up. She sounded almost cheery.

"Don't you understand? I've lost Adrianna. I've lost the woman I love."

"Oh, honey, don't be ridiculous. Adrianna loves you. She simply needs to know you love her, too." His mother rose, stooping to pick up her handbag. "All you have to do is convince her."

CHAPTER TWENTY-ONE

The flowers started arriving shortly after Adrianna got home from work on Friday. By eight, they filled her entire living room. Deep red long-stemmed roses, flirty bunches of daisies in a rainbow of colors, exotic Asiatic lilies.

Even though they didn't come with a card, she knew who'd sent them. She sat in her living room, breathing in the heavenly scents and wondered what Tripp was trying to do.

Impress her? Well, he'd succeeded. Curry her favor? That was harder. Because as much as she loved the fragrant bouquets, that didn't change the fact that she wanted—needed—to occupy the top spot in his heart.

She'd tried to reach him on his cell after the first six bouquets had arrived. Either he deliberately wasn't answering or he was too busy ordering more flowers.

When the doorbell rang, her heart didn't even flutter. It had lurched the first dozen times she'd answered it. Each time it had either been more flowers or a child hawking candy, cookies or popcorn.

Not wanting to get up from the comfortable sofa and her cup

of tea, Adrianna hesitated. When the bell rang again, she heaved a sigh. She rose and grabbed her wallet.

She pulled it open and froze.

Tripp stood on the stoop, a bottle of wine in one hand, a book in another.

"Hi." She managed to push the word past a suddenly dry throat.

"Hi." His blue eyes were dark and watchful. "May I come in?"

She stepped back.

"I brought a bottle of wine." He held up the bottle of burgundy. "Your favorite. I thought we could have some and talk."

"What's there to talk about?" The words were out of her mouth before she could stop them.

His gaze met hers. "A lot."

She shivered. Having him this close was pure torture. He wore jeans and boots and a blue long-sleeved Henley that turned his eyes the color of the sky. He smelled yumm— She stopped herself. "I'll get glasses and a corkscrew."

He was standing by the sofa when she returned from the kitchen. She placed the glasses on the table and took a seat on one end of the overstuffed couch and gestured for him to do the same.

"Thanks for the flowers." She gestured with her hand all around her. "They're, uh, beautiful."

"Not as beautiful as you."

Heat rose up her neck. What was there about this man that turned her into a blushing fool? He expertly uncorked the bottle and poured the burgundy into the glasses. He handed one to her and lifted the other. "I remember everything you said the last time we were together. As you recall, I didn't say much."

Adrianna brought the glass to her lips and took a sip, barely noticing the taste. "What was there to say?"

She glanced down at the book he'd brought, now sitting on

the coffee table. Adrianna lifted it, then tilted her head to one side, puzzled. *"Good to Great?"*

"You've read it."

"A long time ago," she admitted.

"While it's dated, a lot of the concepts still ring true."

"I don't really remember much about it." Adrianna shrugged. "The last time I picked it up was years ago, in a high school business class."

"Let me refresh your memory. The Stockdale Paradox. It's all about retaining unwavering faith that you can and will prevail in the end, regardless of the difficulties."

"Tripp," she interrupted.

"We've had our difficulties." He took a sip of wine. "Because of me."

"There's no point in reliving the past. We—"

"The Hedgehog Concept. It's all about what lights your fire. Where do your passions lie? That one's easy. My passion is you. I love you, Adrianna."

She inhaled sharply, her heart fluttering in her throat. How she had yearned to hear those words from his lips. The moment was bittersweet. "Not as much as you loved Gayle."

"I loved Gayle." His eyes clouded with memories before he blinked them away and his gaze cleared. "But there has always been something between us."

At her protest, he waved a hand. "No, hear me out. You remember that time when I helped you carry those branches out to the street? You were fifteen."

"Fourteen." Even though Adrianna's heart had stopped beating, she still somehow managed to speak.

"It was like you'd touched my soul." He gave a nervous laugh and took a big sip of wine. "I felt a connection to you. I thought you were extremely beautiful. Inside and out."

"I was an ugly duckling."

"Not to me." His voice softened and deepened and when he

reached for her hand she didn't pull away. "When Collins talks about The Flywheel in his book, he says in building greatness, there is no single defining action, no miracle moment."

"You're saying that was when our eyes met?" she managed to stammer.

"That was when the attraction sparked. That wasn't our time. *This* is our time. Or it was, until I got scared and blew it." He expelled a harsh breath, raking his hand through his hair.

"I was frightened you'd never love me as much as Gayle," she admitted. "Never care for me in that same way."

Placing his glass on the coffee table, he reached over and gently cupped her face. "I was scared of losing you. I already cared so deeply. What if you died? How could I bear it?"

"You're not scared anymore?" The words came out in a whisper as Adrianna leaned against his hand.

"I'm terrified." He flashed a quick grin. "But more terrified of not being with you and not sharing a life with you."

Her heart melted to lie in a puddle at her feet. She didn't want to bring up Gayle again, didn't want her to share this moment, but she had to know. "You told your sister Gayle was your soul mate."

He frowned. "I did not."

"You did." She put her own glass down and faced him head-on. "I was standing outside your office and overheard the two of you talking."

His brows furrowed in puzzlement.

"Hailey had been at the hospital for a second interview and—"

"I remember now. When I asked Hailey if she believed in soul mates—" his eyes were clear and very blue "—I was thinking about you, not Gayle."

"Oh." Adrianna blinked before a flood of warmth infused her entire body.

He leaned forward and kissed her. "I love you, Adrianna. So much."

She wrapped her arms around his neck and rested her forehead against his. "I love you, too."

"I have unwavering faith we'll be together forever."

She sat back and smiled. "Another *Good to Great* principle?"

"Stockdale Paradox."

She laughed, giddy with relief and love. "Shut up and kiss me, Tripp Randall. Make it great."

And he did.

EPILOGUE

"There's some kind of mix-up," Adrianna said to Kate Dennes, a local pediatrician and coordinator of this year's Fall Fashion Festival. "I wasn't supposed to wear the wedding dress."

Sponsored by the hospital auxiliary to raise money for new high-tech orthopedic equipment, the black-tie event held at the Spring Gulch Country Club was one of the must-attend social events in Jackson Hole. Some came to see the fashions. Most came because, instead of professional models, the latest fall fashions were showcased by members of the medical community.

Kate lifted her hands, palms up. "The length is too long for Mary Karen, but perfect for someone of your height and stature. It's a necessary change."

There was no way Adrianna could argue with that logic. As she stepped into the strapless dress, Adrianna had to agree Kate had made a wise choice. This gown wouldn't have suited anyone as petite and busty as Mary Karen. The sheath, made of chiffon and charmeuse, hugged her body like a silk glove. It was simple, elegant and unforgiving. Adrianna loved it on sight.

The backstage hairdresser had pulled Adrianna's dark strands into a low chignon set off by intricate fishtail twists and sweeping layers.

"Adrianna," Kate called out just as she slipped on the silver shoes, "you're up."

The gasps from the crowd as she strode out on the stage pleased her almost as much as seeing Tripp's parents and sister beaming at her from the front row. She knew their joy wasn't so much from seeing her as it was from Frank's recent medical report. The new chemotherapy regimen had worked its magic and his cancer was in remission.

She heard Tripp announce her name and relay basic information about the dress to the crowd. Without looking at her, he absently motioned for her to start down the runway. As the emcee of the event, his job was to keep the show moving.

That was why she was surprised when he moved, quick and sleek as a panther in his black tux, from his position to catch her hand when she passed by him.

She smiled and cast him a questioning glance.

When he simply dropped to one knee and pulled a velvet box from his pocket, her heart stopped beating.

"Adrianna," he began, his voice shaking slightly, but clearly audible because of the microphone on his lapel, "I believe God brought me back to Jackson Hole because I was meant to be with you. Your caring and compassion make me strive to be a better person. You bring light into my world and incredible joy. I can't imagine my life without you in it. I love you desperately and I'm hoping you feel the same and want to spend the rest of your life with me. Will you marry me?"

The large ballroom was so quiet you could have heard a pin drop. Then Hailey burst out, "Say yes."

"Yes," Adrianna said softly as joy sluiced through her. "Oh, yes."

Then the ring was on her hand, and when he got back up and swung her around, they were both laughing.

When his lips closed over hers, the room erupted in applause and catcalls.

"Good?" Tripp murmured when they came up for air.

"Great." She hugged him tight. "Definitely great."

I'm so happy you got to enjoy Tripp and Adrianna's story. I'm a huge fan of second chance romances which is probably why I enjoyed writing this book so much. I can see Tripp and Adrianna having a long and happy life together. I especially liked that Adrianna enjoyed a close relationship with Tripp's parents. In real life that isn't always possible but, after experiencing the joys of having wonderful in-laws I'd say it's certainly a bonus.

If you enjoyed this story, you're going to love Healing the Doctor's Heart. In this story a woman who gave up her baby for adoption gets a second chance to be a mother. It has all the same feels as the story you just finished and will leave you with a smile on your face.

Dive into <u>Healing the Doctor's Heart</u> now or keep reading for a sneak peek.

SNEAK PEEK OF HEALING THE
DOCTOR'S HEART

Dr. Kate McNeal sat back in her seat by the front window of Jackson Hole's newest coffee shop, enjoying her cappuccino. It was Saturday and, thanks to a very generous on-call rotation schedule at the pediatrics clinic, she had the whole weekend off.

All Dressed Up and Nowhere to Go could be her motto. Kate sighed and took another sip. Although she'd been in Jackson Hole for almost two years, she had no close friends. Oh, she had tons of social buddies, men and women who invited her to their parties and other events. But no one she felt comfortable calling up on a Saturday morning and asking, "Hey, do you want to grab a scone and then do some shopping?"

Part of the problem was that most of the women she knew had husbands and children. Once she'd reached her early thirties, Kate had discovered there weren't many women left in the single, never-married category. But she couldn't blame her current loneliness *all* on her marital status.

As a child, Kate had been painfully shy. While in her professional life she did fine, shyness was still a struggle in social settings. Worse yet, her reticence often led to her being labeled "aloof" or "standoffish" by those who didn't know her well.

She smoothed the skirt of the buttercup-yellow dress she'd purchased last week. Even though most of the coffee shop patrons were wearing jeans or shorts with a casual shirt, Kate liked to dress up. Wearing stylish things made her *feel* pretty, a feeling that had been in short supply during her growing-up years. Unlike her sister, Andrea, who everyone still raved over, it had taken years for Kate's lanky body to develop a few curves and for her teeth to not look too large for her face.

Back in her early twenties, when she was finally reaching out and becoming the woman she was meant to be, her world had fallen apart. Her grandmother had died. Her boyfriend had deserted her. And she'd had to make a decision no woman should ever have to make…alone. A decision she now lived with every day of her life.

Kate choked down the last bite of lemon-curd scone and gazed out the window, wondering if some shopping therapy would help get her out of this funk.

She was ready to give it a try when she saw Joel Dennes heading toward Hill of Beans, his nine-year-old daughter, Chloe, in tow. Even though she told herself to look away, Kate couldn't take her eyes off them.

Thankfully Joel didn't see her staring. Dressed in jeans and a striped cotton shirt that brought out the green in his hazel eyes, the handsome contractor's entire focus was on his young daughter. Joel was tall—at least six foot two—with a rugged outdoorsy build. His child was petite and slender as a reed with delicate features. From the bag Chloe held, it appeared they'd just come from the dance studio down the street.

So far, on this sunny June morning, Kate had seen at least six little girls walk by with their mothers. Each carried the same type of "dancer" bag she'd once owned.

The normally reserved Chloe let out a peal of laughter at something her father said, and his eyes crinkled with good humor as he settled his hand on her shoulder.

From everything she'd heard and seen, Joel had been doing his best to be both mother and father to Chloe since the death of her mom two years ago.

As far as Kate was concerned, such actions spoke volumes about a man's character. She admired him for stepping up to the plate, admired him a lot.

She shifted in her seat so that her back was to the window, ensuring if they looked her way, she'd simply be a dark-haired woman in a yellow dress.

"Is Joel why you told Ryan you didn't want to see him anymore?"

Kate shifted her gaze to find Lexi Delacourt standing beside her table, latte in hand, wearing a stylish fit and flare dress in green-and-brown. Lexi's dark hair hung loose to her shoulders in a sleek bob. The social worker's amber-colored eyes held a knowing look as her gaze shifted from Kate to the front door. If the bells jingling were any indication, Joel and his daughter had just entered the coffee shop.

"C'mon, Kate, spill." Without waiting for an invitation, Lexi took a seat at Kate's tiny table. "Did you break it off with Ryan because you've got a thing for Joel?"

Lexi and her husband were part of the large ensemble of young professionals that Kate considered "social" friends. They held frequent parties and embraced any opportunity to get together.

Kate's ex-boyfriend, Ryan Harcourt, was part of this group. A former championship bull rider, he had gone on to law school, then returned to his hometown of Jackson to practice. He and Kate had dated until recently when she'd told him she thought it best if they didn't see each other anymore.

In truth, she'd have been content to continue dating him. He was smart, fun and helped fill those lonely hours when she wasn't working. But Ryan had begun to push for a physical and emotional closeness that was more than Kate could give.

Because of her past, she found it difficult to be open even with guys she dated. No, *especially* with guys she dated.

Ryan had given their relationship his all. She'd given it as much as she could, but refused to pretend to have feelings that weren't there.

"Be honest with me," Lexi pressed. "Do you like Joel better than Ryan?"

"It's not that." Kate took a sip of her cappuccino, stalling for time, considering how much to divulge. She hated discussing her personal life. "Ryan and I were—*are*—simply friends."

That much was true.

"His feelings go deeper than friendship." Lexi's eyes never left Kate's face. "I know he really likes you."

Kate fought a surge of irritation. Coming from Pittsburgh and then doing her residency in Los Angeles, she still hadn't completely acclimated to living in a small community. Even though Jackson Hole was a thriving tourist destination, it sometimes felt as if everyone knew everyone's business.

"I realize you and Nick consider Ryan a good friend." Kate chose her words carefully, not wanting to offend. While she might travel in their social circle, she hung on to the fringe by a fingernail while Ryan was firmly woven into the fabric of the group.

"We consider you a friend, too, Kate." As if she'd read her mind, the attractive brunette reached over and briefly covered Kate's hand with hers. "As well as Joel."

The sincerity in Lexi's voice touched Kate's heart. Perhaps she should come clean with the beautiful brunette. It wasn't as if there was any big secret underlying her relationship and breakup with Ryan.

Not like there would be if I dated Joel.

Kate inhaled sharply. *Date Joel?* Where had that thought even come from? Joel Dennes was the last person she'd ever consider dating.

"I'm sorry," Lexi said unexpectedly when the silence lengthened, her cheeks now a bright pink. "It's none of my concern."

"Ryan is a great guy," Kate said honestly. "But you're right. He *was* looking for something more than I wanted out of our relationship."

Ryan had made it clear he was ready to settle down. He'd been convinced he was in love with her. But how could he be? There was so much about her he didn't know.

Lexi gave a little laugh. "That simply tells me he wasn't 'The One' for you."

"The problem wasn't with Ryan." Kate rose to his defense. "It was me. I'm not ready to settle down."

Kate conveniently pushed aside the promise she'd made to herself that when she turned thirty, she'd put her past to rest and move on. That had proven impossible, especially in Jackson Hole.

"If Ryan had been 'The One' it wouldn't have mattered if you were ready or if this was the right time or not."

Kate opened her mouth to argue the point, but Lexi waved her silent.

"Let me tell you a little story." The social worker's hands encircled her cup, the large diamond on her ring finger glittering in the sunlight. "If you'd asked me three years ago why I wasn't in a relationship, I'd have given the same excuse. I was raising Addie on my own and I was content with that arrangement. Then I met Nick."

Kate envied the happiness she saw in Lexi's eyes and heard in her voice, but she wasn't about to get drawn into a discussion about Mr. Right. She focused instead on Lexi's other comment. Even though someone had once mentioned in passing that Nick wasn't their oldest child's biological father, it was easy to forget. "Your ex-husband doesn't live around here, right?"

While she waited for Lexi's answer, Kate took a sip of her cappuccino and noted that Joel and Chloe had gotten their drinks "to go." Obviously they weren't staying. The tightness in her chest eased.

"There is no ex-husband." Lexi's confession pulled Kate back from her thoughts. "Addie's dad and I never married. When Drew found out I was pregnant, he made it clear he didn't want a baby. His career was revving up and he believed having a child would only drag him down. He offered to pay for an abortion."

"Did you ever consider—"

"Not having the baby?" Lexi shook her head. "Never."

"How about adoption?" Although Kate felt her lips move, the words seemed to come from far away.

"It's a great option, but not for me." Lexi's gaze grew thoughtful. "Still, I have to tell you, being a single mom was no walk in the park. Addie and I endured some lean years. When I met Nick, I was working two jobs."

"Not every woman could do that," Kate murmured. The scone she'd just finished eating sat like a dead weight in the pit of her stomach.

"Keeping my daughter was easy," Lexi said, "compared to how hard it would have been to give her up."

Kate could only nod.

"What brings you two fine ladies downtown this morning?"

At the sound of the familiar baritone, Kate's heart plummeted to the tips of her toes. Somehow she managed to lift her gaze and smile.

"I rounded at the hospital early and thought I'd check out Cole and Meg's new business." Even though Kate's heart was above the safe number of beats per minute, thanks to years of practice her tone gave nothing away.

"Chloe and I were just talking about how glad we are that they opened a coffee shop just down the street from The Dance Studio." Joel smiled at his daughter. "We've become Saturday morning regulars."

Kate made a quick mental note *not* to come here again on the weekend, then settled her gaze on the nine-year-old. Chloe's straight dark hair, which normally hung past her shoulders had been pulled back into a makeshift ponytail. Like many preteens, her eyes and teeth seemed too large for her thin face. Although it wasn't obvious to the casual eye, Kate saw the promise of great beauty.

"What do you usually get when you come here?" Lexi bestowed a friendly smile on the two.

"Coffee with cream for me." Joel lifted his cardboard cup. "Nothing fancy."

Even though it would have been easy for him to answer for his daughter, to Joel's credit he merely offered the child an encouraging smile.

Chloe's eyes dropped to the clear plastic cup in her hand. "I got an Italian soda."

"I almost ordered one of those this morning," Kate said, surprising herself by jumping into the conversation. Perhaps because she'd been a shy child and knew how hard it was to have all eyes on you. "My favorite flavor is watermelon."

Chloe lifted her gaze, her eyes wide. "Mine, too."

"Watermelon." Although Joel shook his head in apparent disgust, a smile tugged at her lips. "Must be a girl thing."

Chloe giggled.

For a second, Kate basked in the warmth of the child's pleasure. As Chloe's doctor she'd seen only the little girl's serious side. She'd even spoken with Joel after that first visit about his daughter's reticence, thinking it might be related to her mother's death. But Joel said Chloe had always been shy around strangers.

"Would you like to join us?" Lexi asked. "We could pull up a couple chairs."

Kate remained silent.

Chloe looked up at her father.

Kate held her breath, hoping he would say no, but at the same time wanting them to stay.

"Thanks for the offer," Joel said, sounding sincere. "Unfortunately I have a potential client to meet, so we need to hit the road."

Joel built high-end custom homes in Jackson Hole and from everything Kate had heard, his business was booming despite the economy.

"If that person wants references," Lexi said, "feel free to give them our number. I know Travis and Mary Karen would also be happy to sing your praises."

"Thank you for that. Much appreciated." Joel shifted from one foot to the other, as if embarrassed by the compliment.

Since Joel's Montana-based company had established a presence in Jackson Hole almost five years ago, he'd built homes in the mountains surrounding Jackson not only for Lexi and her husband, but for Mary Karen and Travis Fisher, as well. Kate knew he was in the process of building one for Cole and Meg Lassiter, the couple who owned the shop where they were seated.

"Daddy." Chloe tugged on his arm. "You promised we'd stop and pick up my new ice skates before your meeting."

"You ice skate?" The question popped out of Kate's mouth before she could stop it. If she truly wanted them to leave—which she did—she was doing a poor job of hurrying them on their way.

"Since I was a little girl," Chloe said with a nine-year-old's maturity. "Do you like to skate?"

"I used to," Kate said. "When I was your age."

For her, skating had been a way to forget her troubles at home. She hoped it wasn't that way for Chloe.

"That's cool," Chloe said, then ducked her head, staring down at her hot-pink sneakers.

Joel pulled his phone from his pocket and glanced at it. "We better get going."

From the distant look in his eyes, his thoughts were already on his next appointment.

Kate kept the disappointment she had no right to feel from showing as she watched them walk out the door.

Or at least she *thought* she'd hidden her disappointment.

"His wife hasn't been gone that long. From what I understand they were childhood sweethearts." Lexi took a sip of her latte, a look of sympathy in her eyes. "Give him time. He'll come around."

Kate blinked. "I'm not interested in dating Joel."

"Really?" A tiny smile played at the corners of Lexi's lips. "Could have fooled me."

Even though Kate was absolutely, positively certain she didn't want to date the handsome contractor, she could see where he could catch a woman's eye. "I'll admit he's a good-looking man."

"Oh, you noticed." Lexi looked as if she was trying to keep from laughing. "Even though you're not interested."

After a second Kate chuckled and took a sip of her drink. It was probably best to let Lexi think what she wanted. If she protested too much, her friend's curiosity radar might be activated and she'd ask even more questions.

Questions Kate had no intention of answering.

For now her secret was safe, held close and tight against her heart. And that was just where she intended to keep it.

Grab your copy now of this heartwarming romance now to find out the rest of the story. Healing the Doctor's Heart

ALSO BY CINDY KIRK

Good Hope Series

The Good Hope series is a must-read for those who love stories that uplift and bring a smile to your face.

Check out the entire Good Hope series here.

Hazel Green Series

Readers say "Much like the author's series of Good Hope books, the reader learns about a town, its people, places and stories that enrich the overall experience. It's a journey worth taking."

Check out the entire Hazel Green series here

Holly Pointe Series

Readers say "If you are looking for a festive, romantic read this Christmas, these are the books for you."

Check out the entire Holly Pointe series here

Jackson Hole Series

Heartwarming and uplifting stories set in beautiful Jackson Hole, Wyoming.

Check out the entire Jackson Hole series here

The Driskills of Colorado

A heartwarming new series that brings a small-town feeling to a big city.

Coming Summer 2020

Made in United States
Orlando, FL
16 July 2023

35158953R00143